# A Hitman's Gift For Christmas

NAI

U.A.D PRESENTS

URBAN AINT DEAD

P.O Box 448

Maybrook, NY 12543





Cover Design: P. Wise / The Wise Services

Edited By: Shawna Brim / Ladies of Lit





Contact Author: FB/IG: Authoress Nai / TikTok: @authoressnai / Email: hoodloverssociety@gmail.com

Contact Publisher at www.urbanaintdead.com

Email: urbanaintdead@gmail.com

Print ISBN: 978-1-969593-06-2

# Stay Up to Date

To stay up to date on new releases, plus get information on contests, sneak peeks and more,

Click the link below...
https://mailchi.mp/6d21003686d1/subscribe

# *Soundtracks*

Scan the QR Code below to listen to the Soundtracks/Singles of some of your favorite U.A.D titles:

Don't have Spotify or Apple Music?
No Sweat!
Visit your choice streaming platform and search URBAN AINT DEAD.

Currently on lock serving a bid?
JPay, iHeartRadio, WHATEVER!

We got you covered.
Simply log into your facility's kiosk or tablet, go to music and
search URBAN AINT DEAD.

URBAN AINT DEAD PRESENTS

Like & Follow us on social media:

FB - URBAN AINT DEAD

IG: @uadpresents

Tik Tok - @uadpresents

Submission Guidelines

Submit the first three chapters of your completed manuscript to urbanaintdead@gmail.com, subject line: Your book's title. The manuscript must be in a .doc file and sent as an attachment. The document should be in Times New Roman, double-spaced, and in size 12 font. Also, provide your synopsis and full contact information. If sending multiple submissions, they must each be in a separate email. Have a story but no way to submit it electronically? You can still submit to URBAN AINT DEAD. Send in the first three chapters, written or typed, of your completed manuscript to:

URBAN AINT DEAD
P.O Box 448
Maybrook, NY 12543

*DO NOT send original manuscript. Must be a duplicate.*
Provide your synopsis and a cover letter containing your full contact information.
Thanks for considering URBAN AINT DEAD.

# Author's Note

Wassup, Fine Shiiiiii? So happy to have you back for yet another book where I get ya in and get ya out. I'd like to preface this by saying, this is a novella. The characters will be falling in like IMMEDIATELY. Not because it's a novella but because I believe in falling in love in 2.5 business days. I don't believe it takes long to find your soulmate. I be on some, 'nigga, you don't like green eggs & ham, neither do I. What we naming the baby?' type shit. It's who I am, and I won't apologize for it lmao. That said... I heard y'all, and I'll be getting into those 200 page books in 2026, so stick around. Until then, please enjoy my last novella of the year.

**STAY DELUSIONAL, FINE SHII**

CHAPTER 1

# A Mother First & Foremost

**"T**his little boy gon' make me ring his goddamn neck when I see him, D. I swear."** I gripped my steering wheel tight and pressed my foot harder on the gas to give my truck a little more speed.

It was two in the morning on a Friday night, and here I was, practically flying down the highway to get to the Bronx. The heat in my Range Rover was up, but it had nothing on my anger. I was boiling inside. I had tossed my Moncler coat into the passenger seat an exit ago just to cool off. I even felt my edges sweating under the silk scarf I had on to keep my freshly wrapped quick weave in place. My cousin, Danae, had been trying her best to calm me down via FaceTime, but tonight, her attempts were futile. Tonight, my son, Kaleb Jr., aka KJ, was about to see me in rare form.

Danae often tried to play KJ's savior. He was her godson, and she didn't play about him. We both got on his ass when he went left, but she always drew a line at a certain point – a line that I sometimes had to remind her that I had no problem heel toeing on if I felt the need to. KJ was getting ahead of himself, and it was beginning to be a bit much.

**"Where you at now?"** she asked.

Glancing up at the phone mounted on my dashboard, I could

1

see her snuggled up under her covers. I'd been in the same position thirty minutes ago, watching reruns of *Living Single*, when I realized that my son was playing in my face once again.

**"Just got off the exit,"** I replied.

**"Don't do my boy too bad, Butterfly,"** she reasoned, calling me by my nickname. **"You gotta save your energy for the hoes at the nursing home in a couple hours. You know it takes you a full twenty-four to get your mind right once you're pissed off."**

Shaking my head, I scoffed. **"And so does he. Which is why I don't wanna hear none of that shit tonight, D. Every time I give KJ an inch, he fuck around and take Southern Boulevard. And ever since we moved back up this way, he's been showing his ass. He asked to go chill with his cousins after school. I said cool even though I hate him hanging out in the projects. The stipulation was that he be home by 11 and stay out the way. Here it is, two in the damn morning! I ain't heard from him since four this afternoon. He ain't called, texted, sent a bat signal or nothing. And when I call him, his phone is going straight to voicemail. And you know my rule — that phone should never die."**

**"Yes. I know the rule. And I've always said that it was unrealistic. Phones die, boo."**

**"He has a portable charger,"** I countered.

**"He's a boy. You know how boys can be."**

**"A boy with a 3.8 GPA. He ain't the least bit slow. Slick, yes. But I'ma show his ass who the perm around this motherfucka,"** I vowed.

I'd had plenty of conversations with KJ about keeping me in the loop when he was out, but it seemed like every time he got around his father's side of the family, especially his uncle, he showed his ass. The fact that he was a fifteen-year-old, young, Black man in America wasn't at the forefront of his mind, but it plagued me every time he walked out my front door. I'd been a single mom and divorcee for all of a year. And while being divorced became easier day by day, KJ wasn't making this single parenting shit easy at all.

The closer I got to the projects, the more the streetlights disappeared. The average person would be scared to come through the Bronx at this time of night. I wasn't the least bit fazed. I was on ten and just didn't give a fuck. That and the fact that no matter how much I tried to distance myself from him, people knew who my ex-husband was.

I knew things would be different once Kaleb Sr. got locked up. However, lately it had been feeling like KJ was testing my gangsta, and I didn't like that shit at all. Kaleb had always been the disciplinarian, and while I was no pushover, I never needed to step in because his word was more than enough. Now, I had to show my son that I was indeed Derrick Anderson's daughter – a problem.

**"Well, if his phone is going to voicemail, it's likely dead. I'm not saying don't chastise him when you pull up. Just... take it easy. It's really Koric's ass that's the problem."**

**"Yeah, well, Koric ain't my son. KJ is."**

**"True, but you know KJ only gon' go as far as his uncle lets him while he's over that way."**

She wasn't lying about that, and I had every intention on checking Koric too. Although I knew he loved my son, his ass was a bad influence and always had some shit going on, quite the opposite of his brother – my ex-husband. While Kaleb was quiet and sneaky with his shit, Koric was loud and always in the mix. Kaleb was the mastermind behind a lot of their street dealings, hence the reason he was serving time on a RICO case. It was always something with the Smith men.

**"I'm pulling up to the building now. I'll call you as soon as I make it back home."**

**"Okay. You got your mini me with you?"**

**"Sure do,"** I said, referring to the .380 I had tucked away in my Celine purse.

**"Alright. Don't forget."**

**"I won't. Love you."**

**"Love you too."**

Ending the call, I double parked in front of the building Koric was known to hang out in. Pulling my coat on, I made sure my gun was within reach inside my bag before grabbing it and stepping out of the car. As always, there was a cluster of people mobbing outside, in front of the building, and even more inside the lobby from what I could see, as I stepped onto the sidewalk. It didn't matter that it was freezing outside. Smoke clouded the air as I approached the steps, and as expected, I was greeted with flirtatious catcalls that I ignored.

"Wassup, Ma?" One young boy that looked KJ's age tried it.

"Who you here to see?" another one spoke, cutting his eyes at me and licking his lips.

"It's too late for you to be out here by yaself, boo. Where your man at?" A guy around my age threw his hat in the ring. Still, that didn't stop me from curving him, as I pushed forward.

The crowd parted, and I was face to face with Koric, standing amongst the young boys like he was that nigga – to them at least. He was easy to spot, brown skin with locs braided in his signature four plaits. He shared the same Smith jawline as his brother.

The last time I'd seen Koric in person was a little over a year ago, outside on the courthouse steps the day of Kaleb's sentencing. It was the day everything changed in my marriage. Up until sentencing day, I'd been by Kaleb's side. With my head held high and chest out, I was ready to take on whatever time came our way. It was easy to say "our" because it was the way we operated – as a unit. Partners... or so I thought.

*I sat poised in the first row behind Kaleb in a cream-colored Gucci pantsuit, listening intently, as the state and our lawyer both gave their closing arguments. On the phone this morning, he had forewarned that the odds didn't seem to be in his favor. And although the lawyers on our end had done their jobs, the DA and his team of lawyers and snitches had done theirs better. He was ready to take whatever punishment that was handed down as the face of his operation. "It's what comes wit' this shit," he said.*

*I thought back to his promise of ensuring that KJ and I didn't want for anything in his absence and how I'd told him to save his promise because he was coming home. I believed that wholeheartedly. And even if I hadn't, I'd already promised myself that I wouldn't speak defeat into the atmosphere or to my husband.*

*Then, the judge cleared his throat and spoke. "Kaleb Smith, I hereby sentence you to fifteen years..."*

*Every other word he said sounded muffled after that, like someone had pushed my head underwater. Then there was a wail that echoed from behind me, making everything clear again. The cry had come from a woman, broken and desperate. Turning just enough to see the face behind the theatrics, I noticed a woman of some Hispanic descent dressed in all black with a little girl in her lap. Her hair was in a high ponytail, and each time she rocked, it swung from side to side.*

*The child didn't seem to be affected at all by her outburst, as she lay on the woman's chest. I slowly turned forward and watched as Kaleb's eyes shifted in her direction. His look was stern, a 'cut that shit out' stare that made her go silent, as he was cuffed. Then, his eyes found mine and softened. I stared back, not blinking, appearing completely unmoved, although I was heated.*

*I knew exactly what that outburst signified. It wasn't the cry of a mother who'd just lost her son to the system. It wasn't the cry of a sister who'd just lost her only brother. In fact, the only family ties Kaleb had in the courtroom was me per his instruction.*

*Women didn't cry like that for men they weren't tied to. My chest tightened, the realization hitting me fast. I nodded once, slow and steady, to show him that I understood everything clearly.*

*"I love you, Butterfly," he proclaimed, as he was escorted off to the back to start his new life.*

*I stood, smooth as ever, brushed my hand down my pants, and grabbed my purse. I started up the aisle to the exit and caught a glimpse of the little girl's face. The curve of her cheeks, her sleepy pout, and bushy brows resembled KJ's at that age. Shaking my head, I kept it pushing. My eyes saw what they saw, and I knew what I knew.*

*Leaving the courthouse, I spotted Koric hopping out of a black*

*Acura TL as if he'd been waiting on a cue for my exit. I stepped onto the curb, and he made his way toward me with a Chanel shopping bag in his hand.*

*His expression was unreadable, as he held it out to me. "I'm heading back up top. Bro told me to give you this before I left. Make sure you check the inside. If you or KJ need anything, I'm one call away."*

*I didn't take the bag at first, just cocked my head to the side and stared him down. I never involved Koric in my marriage, but I couldn't help but to ask the question burning in my head. "How old is the little girl?" My voice was clear and unwavering.*

*He didn't flinch or blink, just pushed the bag into my hand and repeated himself. "If you or KJ need anything, hit me."*

*I watched him get back in his car and pull off. Koric didn't know his silence said everything. It was bad enough that my life had been flipped upside down over the last few months from our accounts being frozen to being temporarily barred from my home due to the investigation. It was a lot, but still, I stayed solid, never folding. And not just for Kaleb but for my son, who'd always known his mother to be strong.*

*For the last fourteen years, I'd rode with Kaleb, even in times when I questioned his decision making. Later that night, I opened the bag to find a new Chanel purse. Under normal circumstances, I would've been in awe of the canvas and gold-tone metal shopping bag but not today. Remembering what Koric said about checking the inside, I did and found stacks of wrapped money. Even more significant was the letter, what I considered a rushed apology from Kaleb confessing everything – his two-year affair, the baby that came from it, and a bunch of other bullshit along the lines of 'you don't deserve this' and 'I hope you can find it in your heart to forgive me.'*

*Nigga, what heart? I thought, as I ripped the letter into pieces and threw it in the trash. The judge sealed the fate on Kaleb's future that day, and his lies sealed the fate on our marriage where I left him and his side bitch back in Atlanta.*

I blinked twice, placing myself back in the Bronx, standing in front of Koric surrounded by his minions.

"Where's my son?" I questioned, too irritated to fake a greeting.

"Well, damn, sis. Hey to you too," he replied, smirking. "He's upstairs. Fell asleep in aunty crib. I think his phone dead."

"Your phone dead too?"

"Nah." He reached into his pocket and pulled out an iPhone with a cracked screen. "I'm charged up," he said, like he was reporting good news.

"You think that's funny, Koric? You think I came out in the dead of winter to joke witchu?"

"Damn, K," a young boy snickered from the crowd, "she on yo' ass."

Koric looked past me, and his eyes turned to slits. "Aye, Rome, you minding family business?"

I'd known him to be a lunatic, and by the bewildered look on the boy's face, he knew it too. I wanted to save him the embarrassment and Koric's wrath.

"Nah. Nah, I ain't," the kid let out in a nervous tone.

"Can we talk without the crowd?" I suggested.

"Yeah," Koric agreed, eyes never leaving the kid. After a few seconds of a menacing stare down, he gestured toward the building.

"Look, Koric, I'm well aware that you have these young boys out here marching to the beat of your drum, but when it comes to KJ, he has rules, and I have standards," I expressed once we separated from the group. "I don't want my son out on the block getting involved in shit he knows nothing about. I don't understand why I gotta tell you that as his uncle."

"You ain't gotta tell me that though, Thyri. I don't involve KJ in shit I got going on. You came out here late cause you wanted to. He wit' his people. You know we ain't gon' let shit happen to him. You be stressin' over shit that ain't that deep."

"Ain't that deep?" I repeated. "No, everything is that deep when it comes to my child. And the fact that it's after two in the morning and I'm standing in front of the projects going back-and-forth witchu makes it deep as fuck. Call my son downstairs so I can go please."

"Aight, Thyri. I'm not 'bout to be out here arguing with my brother's wife. Lemme call up there."

"Yeah. You do that. And I'm not your brother's wife."

"Yeah, well, tell that nigga that," he countered before placing a call to whoever on his phone.

A few minutes later, KJ suddenly appeared with his bookbag on his back, rubbing his tired eyes. His face fell when he saw me. He already knew what time it was.

"Ma…"

"The car," I said, turning away from him and walking back down the steps. I wanted to say so much more, but I wasn't a fan of embarrassing my child – no matter how bad I wanted to go across his shit.

I could hear him and Koric exchange goodbyes before he followed me to the curb. As I reached the driver's side, I caught him trying to hop in the backseat.

"Nah." I stopped him. "Get yo ass right in the front. You did the crime, now you gon' hear my mouth thee whole way home."

With a look full of disdain, he pulled the passenger door open and plopped down in the seat. Seeing the look on his face, I warned him before he closed the door.

"If you slam my door, you gon' have an even bigger problem than you have now. Close it the fuck soft," I warned through clenched teeth, mimicking the social media influencer, Supa Cent. Had the situation not been serious, I would've cracked up laughing at myself.

Taking heed to my warning, he did just that. Snapping his seatbelt, he turned to the window, as I sped off from the curb.

"Ma," he called out after the couple minutes of silence I let him stew in.

"KJ," I replied, not taking my eyes off the road.

"I'm so…"

"No," I cut him off, "you don't get to *I'm sorry* your way out of this one. Tonight, you played yourself. I give you a chance to prove to me that you can be responsible, and you just showed me the reason I gotta stay on yo' ass. It ain't no way you got me out my bed at this time to come and look for you!"

"I ain't even do nuffin'," he muttered.

"You right. You ain't do nuffin'," I repeated the same way he had. "You ain't do nuffin' I told yo' ass to do."

"Ma, I was chillin'. We played basketball for a few then went upstairs to play the game. I ate and fell asleep. At some point, my phone died, and I didn't realize it. You can ask Uncle Koric."

"I'm not asking Koric shit. I'm not responsible for Koric. Koric don't live under my roof. KJ does. Koric don't have to follow my rules. KJ does. And what is the number one rule when you're out, Kaleb Maurice Smith?"

"Don't let my phone die," he grumbled.

"And your phone is currently what?"

"Dead."

"Exactly. Hence the reason we're here."

Slouching deeper into his seat, he sucked his teeth. "I told you I fell asleep when the phone died."

Slamming on the brakes at a red light, I reached over and grabbed a fistful of his coat. "First of all, you ain't **tellin'** me shit. Watch your tone and posture when you talkin' to me, KJ. Don't let me being an understanding mother fool you. We can box."

"Aight, Ma. My bad."

"Mmmhmm. Yeah." Loosening my grip, I pushed him in his chest and pulled off at the green light. "And just so there's no misunderstanding, you're grounded."

He sucked his teeth again. "Ma, forreal? Come on, the season just started. I got practice."

KJ was a star player on his school's basketball team. It was the one thing he loved most besides me and his father. Up until our move back to New York last year, I hadn't had any issues with him other than normal teenage stuff. He was a straight A student, polite, and respectful. But when his father went away, a part of him changed. While the grades and his love for basketball remained, he'd picked up a new interest – the streets. And I knew it was the sole reason he wanted to be around Koric more.

"You can still go to practice. Me or your godmother will be there to pick you up every day at six."

"Pick me up?! That's embarrassing."

"Unfortunately for you, son, compromises are on hold at the moment."

By the time we made it back home to Manhattan, my anger had subsided, and exhaustion had kicked in. KJ had his hand on the door handle before I could shift the car in park. The whole afterschool pick up was not ideal for him. I couldn't think of a better punishment than to temporarily strip him from his independence. Entering our apartment, I kicked off my shoes at the door and hung up my coat.

"Goodnight, KJ," I said to him, as he beelined toward his room. "I love you."

"Love you too," he forced out.

Shaking my head, I sent Danae a text to let her know we'd made it home and that I'd call her later. She responded back that KJ had already texted her. I chuckled at him calling himself telling on me. Exiting the text thread, I navigated to my email. I'd set up a profile on Care.com a couple days ago for a nanny position and had yet to hear back. I needed something to do with myself a few days out of the week when I wasn't visiting with my father in the rehabilitation center, and being that I loved kids, I figured why not.

Typing Care.com into the search, nothing popped up from the site, but one email did catch my eye. It was from a company by the name of SULLIVAN & CO with the subject: Care.com Nanny Inquiry. Knowing I wasn't going to send a response at this time of night, I moved the email to my high priority folder to check in a few hours. Right now, I needed sleep.

## CHAPTER 2

# The Weight of The Morning

After getting a few hours of sleep, I woke up, expecting to hear KJ moving about the house, getting ready for school. Only the house was quiet. And he was everything but that during the morning hours. Rolling over, I reached for my phone to check the time and was greeted by a text notification from him.

Sonshine: Went to school.

The text was dry and forced. No "good morning" in the opening and no "I love you" at the end. Typical teenage boy shit. That didn't stop me from responding as a mother – a Black mother.

Me: Good morning, son. I implore you to keep this same energy for Christmas in the next two weeks. My pockets have been begging for a break. See you at 6 p.m. sharp. Have a productive day. I love you.

The three dots jumped across the screen like he was going to respond then disappeared. He must've had second thoughts about what he wanted to say, and that was a good thing. I didn't have the capacity to go back-and-forth with an emotional teenage terrorist anyway.

Setting my phone back down on my nightstand, I pulled my comforter from my body and sat up straight. The muscles in my neck ached from the way I slept, so I headed straight for the shower. Stripping out of my clothes, I turned the water on as hot as I could stand it and stepped inside. As the hot water beat down on my back, I rolled my shoulders, feeling some of the tension releasing from my muscles. This shower was longer than usual. The moment of solitude was needed.

Soaping up twice and rinsing off, I wrapped a towel big enough to fit two people around my body. Wiping the steam from the mirror, I stared back at my reflection. The last year had been an adjustment that I hadn't seen coming, and the sudden need to pivot had taken a toll on me mentally, but I was grateful that it didn't show up in my appearance. My rich brown complexion was still bright, and my eyes were void of bags. That was a blessing.

Grabbing my facial wash, I began my ten-minute skin routine that kept me blemish free and many suitors questioning my age. Once I achieved that perfect, glass look, I brushed my teeth and headed into the closet. Quickly deciding on a cute but comfy look for the day, I put on a pair of fitted jeans, a cream-colored sweater, and slid my feet into a pair of Bottega sneakers. Today was a routine visit with my father at the nursing home. Like any other day, I prayed that I wouldn't get there and have to wake the whole facility up about my daddy.

Fully dressed, I made up my bed, checked KJ's room to make sure his was made up, then headed for the kitchen to put something on my stomach. There was no telling when I'd stop to eat once I got moving. Passing by the living room, I glanced over at the Christmas decorations I'd taken out and made a mental note to start putting stuff up later today. My Christmas tree stood tall in all its green glory, equipped with a tree skirt but not one ornament in sight. I'd been waiting on KJ to partake in ornament hanging, but he'd been so wrapped up in KJ land that I thought he'd missed the tree being up.

If I was honest, I wasn't in the Christmas spirit this year. I hated that for me because this was **my** holiday. It was customary that my tree was up and the house gave Winter Wonderland the day after Thanksgiving. Not this year. I wasn't feeling it for many reasons. I'd hoped that my father would be home by now, but we were still working at his rehab to get him more stable after his stroke. Add on KJ's schedule and keeping him on the right track, recovering from divorce, and navigating my new life as well as finances, it was a lot on ya girl. But still, I rise.

After a quick breakfast of rye toast, turkey sausage, and a cup of chai tea, I loaded the dishwasher and packed my bag for the day. I planned to spend most of the day with my father, so I grabbed my iPad, journal, along with my wallet, keys, and phone. Tossing everything into my Glamaholic tote bag, I combed my hair out and put on one of my puffer coats to fight the wind. On my way out, I snatched up my Brümate cup and a pack of granola. In my car was a dad kit that I always restocked after a visit with my father – a track suit, fresh underclothes, and toiletries. Though he had things at the rehab facility, the staff did a piss poor job of doing what I asked in a timely manner, so it was my job to make sure that my father was up to par.

Getting in my car, I started it. While the engine warmed up, I connected my phone to call Danae. Before I could tap her contact from my favorites, my phone rang with an incoming call. The screen read Kaleb Sr. His contact had been listed under Disloyal Bastard up until a few months ago. And that was because KJ had pointed it out as a joke. I never wanted my son to see me as bitter, so I changed it quick.

I kept my communication brief with Kaleb. KJ was a young adult who could report anything he had going on directly to his father. If there was something I needed handled regarding him, I made sure that we discussed it during our first of the month debriefing. Those calls were brief and consisted of me confirming that I'd received the funds for rent and any expenses related to KJ that he hadn't already given him directly. We'd had that call for

December already, so I was curious to know why he was on my line now.

Sighing, I answered. **"Hello."**

**"Wassup, wifey?"** he greeted jovially, quite the opposite of a man serving time.

**"Not your wifey. How can I help you, Kaleb?"**

Silence hung in the air before he answered. He was likely trying to gauge my mood. **"I wanted to hit you to see if you had time to go over what we getting KJ for Christmas."**

I rolled my eyes. **"We not getting him anything. You do you, and I'ma do me. Then we meet in the middle and make sure it's a success. We don't need to discuss it. KJ is fifteen."**

He let out an audible sigh and blew out a breath. **"Why you gotta make it difficult to talk to you, Thyri?"**

**"I'm not,"** I countered. **"You're just used to handling me as your wife and not the co-parent. Thyri the wife was more open to compromise and how things could accommodate you. Thyri the co-parent does what she feels is best and what ultimately works for her."**

**"Well, tell Thyri the co-parent that she's making co-parenting more difficult than it needs to be. I'll get with KJ to see what he wants and have Koric bring it over. Does Thryi mind wrapping the gifts?"**

**"Thyri can... for the low price of $100,"** I said seriously while pulling out of my parking spot.

**"You love taxing a nigga."**

**"Hey, alimony wasn't a part of the divorce package, so it is what it is. Will that be all?"** If I didn't bring the conversation to a close, Kaleb would try to hold me hostage.

**"I heard you were in the Bronx earlier this morning. What was that about?"**

**"Kaleb, if you're asking, then you already know the answer."**

**"I do. I just wanted to hear your logic for showing up in the projects that late, like shit ain't always popping off over that way."**

"It's exactly why I went to get our son who I hadn't heard from."

"Need I remind you that he was with my family? And he's a fifteen-year-old young man who can handle himself."

"You don't get to monitor my parenting from behind the wall, Kaleb. I have no doubt that KJ can handle himself, but so long as he's under my roof, he'll do what I ask to avoid me making trips to the projects."

"He can't grow into a man if you don't let him bump his head a few times, Thyri."

"Yeah, well, a man keeps his word and handles his responsibilities. KJ gave me his word on something and did not follow through. If I gotta hold his ass to the fire about it, whoopty doo. The last thing I wanna do is go back-and-forth with you about it. Can I go now?"

If I let him, Kaleb would argue me down for forty days and forty nights about anything he deemed argument worthy.

Again, he went quiet.

"I don't want you to think that just because I'm in here means that I'm not looking after our son wherever he is. That goes for you too. All I'm saying is you pulling up like that in the wee hours of the night is dangerous and needs not to happen again."

"Until you have a conversation with KJ about how he moves, I'll be doing what I have to do when I have to do it. I gotta go."

"I can do that. Have a good day, Butterfly. I love you."

I ended the call without responding. I knew I was pushing it with the way I was speaking to him. A part of me felt like Kaleb was letting me get away with it because he still felt guilty about the demise of our marriage. And he fucking should. Fumbling me was the worst thing he could have ever done. Now, I had an attitude and didn't feel like calling Danae. Instead, I drove in silence, wanting to shake off my anger before I got to my dad.

After an almost two-hour drive, I arrived at Parker Jewish Institute in Queens. The nursing home looked good on the outside, but on the inside, the care was mediocre, at least when it came to my standards for my father. However, it was still considered the best out of the ones in his area that we had to choose from at the time. I silently hoped that today wasn't one of those days where I had to go off on anybody about his care plan. Well, the care plan I'd set for him.

While I expected them to be as unorganized as they usually were, what I saw instead had me seeing red and fighting back tears at the same time. My father was sitting in his wheelchair, in the middle of his room, in front of the TV, in nothing but a blanket and his boxers.

No socks. No t-shirt. Nothing.

He sat in the chair with his head hung low, likely from embarrassment, and his legs shaking from cold air. This was my daddy, my fucking hero, that they had sitting here practically naked with no one around. Tears filled my eyes, as I dropped his bag and walked around to kneel in front of him.

"Daddy." My voice cracked.

His head lifted slowly, acknowledging my presence with a faint smile. But I could sense his discomfort and vulnerability, a far cry from the strong man I grew up with. A stroke had taken my daddy's independence, and now these bitches were trying to strip him of his dignity. I bit my lip, doing my best to fight the tears threatening to fall. I didn't want him to think I wasn't strong enough to handle things.

"Gimme one second, Daddy. Lemme see what the hell is going on." I wrapped the blanket fully around his body for temporary comfort, kissed his forehead, and stormed out into the hallway.

I looked both ways before charging over to the nurses' station where I found a few nursing aides standing around, talking amongst themselves.

"Excuse me!" I snapped, breaking up their powwow.

They all turned in my direction, but only one spoke. "Yes. Is there something that you need?"

"Yes. I need for y'all to get on y'all fuckin' job! While y'all over here in a huddle, my father is sitting in his room practically naked!"

"Ms. Anderson." I heard my name and turned to see a nurse rushing down the hall to my father's room with a cart. "I'm taking care of him right now."

"She'll handle it," the woman in front of me said, like she was dismissing me.

"Yes, she will and so will the D.O.N. Call her down here to speak to me, or she can speak to my lawyer when I sue y'all ass. Y'all got me and my daddy fucked up. Play with me if y'all want to." With my promise to nut the fuck up in the air, I returned to my father's room where the nurse was pulling his clothes out of the small closet.

"I just stepped out for a minute to take care of another patient after they brought him in from the shower. I wasn't gone lo..."

"I don't give a damn about nobody else in this place but this man right here." I tapped my father's back. "Every time I come here, y'all got an excuse for y'all negligence. Not today! There's no excuse for this shit. You can go. I'll dress him myself."

"Ms. A..."

"Miss, I'm letting you off easy. Please get out before you have to see what it's like to be the patient."

Clear on the threat to her health, she took her cart and scurried out.

I could hear my father clearing his throat before calling out my name. "Thy...ri," he made out slowly.

His voice still had a heavy slur to it after the stroke. While other people struggled to understand him, his words were always clear enough for me. It was my job to know what he was trying to convey, even if it took him a minute to get the words out.

"Gimme one second, Daddy," I said, still facing away from him, so he wouldn't see me crying. I wiped at my eyes with the back of my hand and took a breath to collect myself. "Let me get you some clothes."

"O...kay."

I was the definition of a daddy's girl. And for most of my

teenage years, it had always been me and him. My mother had been in the picture up until their divorce. She took it hard and decided that she couldn't bear to live in the same state as the man who broke her heart, so she moved. I had a choice to go with her or stay, and to be honest, I didn't know why she even asked. I couldn't fathom moving and leaving my daddy behind.

My mother didn't fight for me, nor did she force me to leave. She just packed up, said she loved me, and moved. Eventually, she moved on. She got remarried and had my little sister, Tiya. I visited with them in the summer, but it was clear that my mother and I would never share a bond as tight as me and my dad's. I didn't love her any less, and she didn't treat me any different than my sister. That was smart on her part because my daddy would've let her have it if she did.

He was my guy, a hardworking man who was good with his hands. I called him Mr. Fix It because, somehow, he always knew his way around a tool, and not just the common ones. He taught me how to ride a bike. Taught me how to cook. Taught me how to shoot a gun and how to keep shit P before it was even a thing.

But the best thing my father could have ever taught me was how to be resilient and to always remember that I was the prize. It was the strength that he instilled in me and his constant words of encouragement that held me up, as I went through my divorce. He never threw dirt on Kaleb's name or even spoke on what happened at the time. He just held his daughter down like the hero he was.

Before Kaleb and I made our move down to Atlanta, my father was fine. Still the life of any party, still teaching KJ to box while giving him lessons on financial literacy and still coming by my house to find something to fix just to spend time with me. Then the stroke happened not long after I moved back to New York and altered our lives. It hit me hard. But it hit him harder. My dad was an independent man who lived a full life and was used to taking care of people. To now be on the receiving end wasn't ideal for him under the circumstances.

"It's...cold...as...hell..." he murmured.

"I know, Daddy. I got you." Pulling the blanket from his body, I carefully put on his thermals with the track suit I'd bought in the bag.

He did his best to help me help him, and all I could do was smile to show my appreciation. Having him move around as much as he could with me was my way of doing my own physical therapy with him.

"Put your foot up for me, so I can put your socks on, Daddy." He did as I asked, and once he was warm and settled, his hand touched mine.

"Thank you." He flashed a crooked smile and squeezed my fingers weakly.

"You don't have to thank me, Daddy. You know your babygirl got you. And just as soon as Nurse Monarch get in here, I'ma let her ass have it. You know I'll go to war about the best father in the world."

His eyes softened again, and he nodded slowly. "I...lo...ve you, Thy...ri." His eyes welled up, and something broke in me.

"I love you too, Daddy. I'm moving you outta here," I told him. "I promise it'll be soon. You're gonna come home with me and KJ. Just give me some time to get everything situated. Hold on a little bit longer for me. I'm gonna handle everything."

I wrapped my arms around him, holding him tight. I knew the process of getting him home and set up with the continued rehab he needed would be no easy feat, but I also knew if I kept him at the rehab facility any longer, I'd be in prison. So, it was time for me to go into hustle mode. While it would be easy to just get the money from Kaleb, I didn't want his help to come with stipulations. I was gonna take care of mine.

## CHAPTER 3

# A Hitman & His Baby Boy

By the time I walked through my door, it was after three in the morning. Tonight's job ended up being more work than I was contracted for, setting me back an hour. Still, it got done, and I put a heavy tax on the initial price to compensate me for my time. No one ever had a problem paying; no one wanted the energy that a problem with me could bring anyway. Quickly arming the alarm, I made my way down my dimly lit hallway.

Dressed casually in an Essentials sweatsuit, one wouldn't have known that I'd just killed two men execution style, as they loaded a truck with stolen ki's in the dead of night. It was usually some form of torture for thieves, but I'd been given the contract at the last minute, so two shots to the head from my Barrett MRAD did the trick. After every job, I stopped at my duck off apartment to change, clean, and break down my weapon of choice. In my line of work, it was important to be as discreet as possible and always keep the business far away from family. Following those rules kept me sane and my loved ones alive.

When I stepped into my house, I was Enzo aka Ezzy, the loving single father and businessman – not the calculated killer I'd been hours ago. Walking farther into the house, I could see the light from the kitchen on and heard the TV playing lowly. Inside, my mother sat at the kitchen island with a bottle of XXL wine, watching the cooking channel. Her terrycloth robe was tied tight, and she had her scarf tied around her head like Prince, keeping her silk press in place.

"EJ must've done a number on you for you to pull out the cheap shit. That bottle been sitting in the fridge since Thanksgiving. I've been meaning to give it back to Aunt Rozalyn."

"Shiidd, I'm sure glad it was in there because no bottle of Merlot could settle me after dealing witcho bad ass son. I'm too old to be compromising with a two-year-old about what time he gon' go to bed."

Chuckling, I walked over to kiss her forehead. "My boy drove you crazy, huh?"

She drew her head back in offense. "Drove me crazy? That lil' goddamn Tasmanian Devil was almost on the damn ceiling at one point. You need to bottle all his energy up and sell it. I had to check his multivitamins to make sure he ain't have no Adderall mixed in before giving it to him."

I leaned over the counter, laughing. "All two-year-olds don't have that kind of energy, Ma?"

"No. EJ is different. He'll take yo' ass on an adventure without having to leave the house. And he slick like you. Soon as I get to yelling, he flash that innocent look and do that, 'Okay, Grandma'." She mimicked his voice, down to the way he hung his head when he was in trouble, making me laugh harder. "It ain't funny." She chuckled, taking a sip of her wine. "I know a terrorist when I see one."

"Don't do my lil' man like that, Ma."

She sighed and set the wine glass down. "On a serious note though, Enzo. You need help. Real help. And you know I love my grandbaby, but he needs someone more physically active to be here with him when you're out. Now, I get how you feel about the daycares, and I know you want to be super dad." She reached over and squeezed my hand. "Mama not taking that from you at all. I'm just saying you need more help."

Exhaling through my nose, I ran my hand over my waves. She wasn't wrong. I did need help with EJ – not because I couldn't handle it but because my schedule was unpredictable. Unfortunately, I couldn't take him everywhere.

"You're right," I admitted. "I actually responded to a Care.com ad."

Her eyebrows jumped. "Wait. Not you taking my advice. I just knew it went in one ear and out the other when I mentioned it to you weeks ago."

"It did." I chuckled. "But I don't wanna be inconsiderate of your time or anyone else's. I sent the message yesterday, just waiting on a reply."

"Did you review the profile?"

I nodded. "Yeah. She seems legit. She has genuine eyes too. They actually remind me of Grandma Lettie's. I think that's what made me send the email."

I thought about the brown skinned woman in the profile picture that wore a subtle smile. It was inviting yet reserved.

She smirked. "Interesting. Well, I hope it works out then. It don't make sense with as big as our family is; nobody besides me is able to watch him for more than a few hours."

Smiling, I shrugged. I knew my son was more than a handful. He wasn't bad to me though. Just wild as fuck.

Downing the rest of her wine, my mother stood and stretched slowly. "I made baked chicken, wild rice, and broccolini. Your plate is in the fridge. Sonic The Hedgehog cleared his plate and had me make him a bowl of oatmeal like it was a side dish. He had a bath too. I'm going to bed. I got a long day of relaxation ahead of me."

"Oh, yeah? What you got going on?"

"Spa day with my sisters." She smiled. "Then we going to the casino."

"Ahhh, shit. How much you need?"

"Nothing. Your cousin, Aura, is sponsoring the whole thing. It's another one of his birthday gifts to his mom."

"Oh, that's wassup. Better him than me."

She turned to me with her hand up on her hip. "Says the kid who used to shake his piggy bank and everybody else's to make sure he always got me something special for Mother's Day. Boy, you know you'd spend your last on yo' mama."

"Five times over." I kissed her cheek again and picked up her wine glass to walk over to the sink and turn off the TV.

"And that's one of the many reasons Mama love you. Night, son. And you make sure you pray before you close your eyes tonight. I can tell you were out there doing something not pleasing unto the Lord. I love you."

I didn't need to respond. She knew the family business and the role I played. She just pretended not to for her own reasons. I was a hitman for the Sullivan family, the Black Mafia if you would. Our street dealings went back to the 60s. We were mainly based in New York, although our reach extended way past that.

But I wasn't just a hired hitta, and the Sullivan family wasn't just associated with illegal activity. We all owned legitimate businesses as well, mine being Sullivan and Co., a cleaning service that specialized in residential housekeeping, cleaning of office buildings, and laundry services for different wedding venues within the five boroughs. I also had a VIP cleaning service that was… off the books. Whether legal or illegal, I was a busy man. And even though I still made time to be a present father, EJ needed more.

My mother disappeared into the guest bedroom, while I made my way down the hall, stopping at EJ's room across from mine. Pushing the door open quietly, I smiled. My lil' man was knocked out with his feet hanging off the side of his car themed bed. By the way he slept, I could tell he'd run himself ragged. He looked nothing like the Tasmanian Devil that my mother described. He looked innocent. Peaceful.

His durag was neatly tied over a fresh set of twists, just as I'd left it earlier in the day. Walking into the room, I carefully pushed him up so that his body was on the bed fully and covered him with his comforter. Satisfied that he was snuggled enough, I stared down at him. God hadn't just given me a son but the greatest responsibility of my life. I'd been raising EJ alone since the day he was born – since the day his mother decided that if I didn't feel that she was good enough to be my wife, she wasn't going to reduce herself to just being my child's mother. She gave me the ultimatum only a few hours after our son was born in an effort to force me to propose.

Kennedy didn't know it, but her actions proved why she wasn't cut out to be the wife of a man of my caliber, let alone the mother of my son. She didn't deserve us, so I freed her of her duties before they even began. I thanked her for birthing a legacy she'd never get to see grow and promised that if she ever came back around, trying to disrupt my son's quality of life, I'd be sure to end hers. It was just that simple to me then.

Now, as I watched him sleep, I felt a mixture of love and anger. I loved my son more than I loved myself, but my anger came from a small part of me believing I'd done him a disservice by depriving him of a mother. Sometimes I wondered what the last two years would've looked like had I made her stay. If I'd sacrificed my happiness for a life of contentment and a forced marriage, would things be different now? Then, I could hear my mother's words the day we brought EJ home.

*"Just because Kennedy selfish ass gave birth, it doesn't make her a mother. She made her decision. And you may be sparing your son a lifetime of heartache by letting her go. A son's first heartbreak is usually by his mother."*

I bent down and kissed the crown of his head.

"Daddy got you," I whispered. "Always."

Straightening, I looked around his room once more before heading to mine. The shower was my next stop. I stepped into the hot water and let it wash away the sins that I could never speak on out loud. Closing my eyes, I lifted my head, and the water poured down my face. Pressing my hands to my face, I recited my nightly prayer for God to forgive me for any area in my life that wasn't pleasing to him. While I knew God knew my heart, I also knew there was that side of me that he wanted to deliver me from. He was just waiting on me to be ready.

After twenty minutes, I got out of the shower, dried off, and pulled on a pair of pajama pants. Setting the temperature in my room to 74 degrees, I turned the ringer off on both of my phones and slid into bed. The woman from the Care.com ad crossed my mind. I hoped that she responded soon and even more that she'd be a good fit for me and EJ. Exhaling, I closed my eyes, sleep coming almost immediately. Something told me that tomorrow would bring good news that would shift things for us.

---

I WOKE up to the sounds of my TV and EJ sitting on the foot of my bed with his robe on, his legs crossed, and his eyes glued to *Cars*. It was his favorite movie and his ritual to watch it at least once a day. His durag was still on his head but slightly crooked, indicating he'd had a good night's rest. Rubbing sleep from my eyes, I tapped his back with my foot.

"Good morning, lil' man."

He didn't respond back but turned around and looked down at my foot like he was trying to figure out why I had it on him.

"My bad, dawg." I chuckled, sitting up. "Good morning, man."

"Daddy, Lighten Mc-Keen. Look." Mispronouncing the words proudly, he pointed to the TV.

"It's McQueen, EJ," I corrected, stretching. "Say, McQueen."

"McKeen," he repeated incorrectly.

"Shiiiddd, if you wanna go around sounding crazy, that's on you. They may let you slide cause you two though. You might be straight."

Nodding like he understood and was completely fine with my logic, he turned back to the TV and turned the volume up by exactly one bar. I chuckled inwardly. Last week, I'd told him that the TV couldn't be too loud in the morning and showed him how many bars the volume could be on to make sure it wasn't. And EJ followed directions as he normally did – like he normally did with me anyway.

Propping up on the headboard, I watched him watch TV, getting excited by the same scenes he'd seen countless times. The door to my bedroom opened, and my mother walked in fully dressed in a turtleneck, jeans, and shoe boots.

"You look nice, Ma," I complimented.

"Thank you, baby." She pointed to EJ. "His oatmeal is on the counter cooling off, and his chocolate milk is in the fridge." Walking into the room, she leaned over and kissed his forehead. "Grandma love you, bad ass." She then kissed my cheek. "I made enough for him to have two bowls and you to have one. I gotta get going."

"Rushing to leave your two favorite guys is crazy. We gon' be aight though. Ain't that right, EJ?"

EJ looked at his grandma, then to me, then back to the TV.

"Exactly." She giggled. "He don't give a damn. I gotta get out of here. We're carpooling, and I don't wanna be late."

"Aight." I laughed and reached for my personal phone on the nightstand. "Have a good time. I love you and check your CashApp when you get a chance."

"What you done sent me, Enzo?" Pulling her phone out of her purse, she shook her head. "I told you I didn't have to pay for nothing today."

"I know that. Just consider it a thank you for you coming through last minute yesterday and watching EJ. I appreciate it."

She gave me a soft smile. "Y'all my babies. That's my job. No thanks needed for loving what's mine. But I appreciate you too, son. I'll put this money to good use at the 'sino." Waving, she left the room.

My mother always had good luck at the casino, so there was no doubt in my mind that she'd double the $500 I'd sent her.

"Aye, Champ. Come on, let's go brush our teeth and eat breakfast."

EJ heard food and slid off the bed with ease, landing on his feet. He trailed behind me, walking as fast as his little legs would allow to keep up. Grabbing my toothbrush from my bathroom, I went into his to brush my teeth. Familiar with the routine, he grabbed his step stool to place it at the sink and climbed up on it. I always found myself fascinated by the things he remembered.

"O'meal," he said once we were done.

"I got you. Come on."

Heading into the kitchen, I set him up at the table and grabbed his bowl off the counter.

"Aye," I said, "you know the rule. Whatever you spill, you gon' clean up. Copy?"

He stared at me seriously before nodding. Clear that we were on the same page, I slid the bowl in front of him.

"And take ya time," I added, handing him a small spoon.

I got another nod of understanding, and he dug in. We ate together in silence, him clearing his bowl before me and holding it up for seconds. Oatmeal was his favorite meal – specifically, the way my mama made it. I didn't know what special ingredient she added, but his lil' ass was hooked. I tried my hand at perfecting it and failed miserably. The way he projectile vomited let me know that. After breakfast, I cleaned him up, and we retired to the living room.

"You wanna help Daddy put the Christmas tree up, man?"

His face lit up, and he jumped down off the couch, headed for the closet where he'd seen me stash the tree. Chuckling, I stood, walking over to the closet to drag the big box out. Making room in the corner of the living room, we got to work. By the look on his face, it was clear that EJ was taking his job of handing me each branch seriously. He concentrated so hard, checking each branch before handing it over to me.

"Aight, what you think?" I asked once the ornaments were on. His response was a frown, as he shook his head. "What? It's missing something?" I checked the tree out and thought we'd done a good job.

"Light," he said, pointing at the tree.

"Ohhhh, got you." I plugged the cord in the socket, bringing the tree to life, as it lit up.

His eyes got big. "Good job."

"Yeah. We did it. Good job, man. Here, this the last thing." I handed him a star and picked him up to place it on top of the tree. "Gimme some dap."

Slapping fives with me, he laid his head on my shoulder. This was life. Me and my baby boy.

Satisfied with our tree, we made our way to his playroom where I let him run off his breakfast, while I checked my emails. In scrolling through my inbox, I found a response email to my nanny inquiry. Clicking on it, I read in silence.

*From: Thyri.Anderson@gmail.com*

*Good afternoon, Mr. Sullivan,*

*Thank you for your response. My current availability is Tuesday-Friday and alternate weekends from 8 a.m.- 4 p.m. While a set schedule would be ideal, I can be flexible when needed. I'd love to schedule an in-person meeting to discuss further if possible. Please let me know what day and time works best for you.*

For some reason, I found myself reading the email twice. The message was the same, but I was trying to put a voice to the words.

"Type shit I'm on?" I silently questioned myself before responding.

*From: Sullivan & Co*

*Good morning, Ms. Anderson,*

*Are you available this afternoon at 12:30 p.m.? If so, you can meet me at this address, 22 Chambers Street New York, NY. Let me know if this works for you.*

I sent the email, and she replied a few minutes later that she'd be there. That was already a plus in my book. It let me know she wanted to work, and that said a lot. Powering off my laptop, I tucked it under my arm and stood up from the bean bag chair I sat on.

"Come on, EJ, let's get dressed. We got an interview."

I dressed us both in matching cargo pants and black crew neck sweaters. On our feet were a fresh pair of black Timbs. Of course, he had to break his in by taking a couple laps around the house. My boy was the miniature version of me. Hitting my body with a few sprays of cologne, I sprayed some in the air and let him run through, so he could smell good too.

"Go get your coat and your hat, EJ," I directed. Taking flight, he did as I asked and came running back, tripping over his own feet along the way. "Woah, slow down, dawg." I held my hand out to his chest, only for him to laugh.

"I running, Daddy."

"I know." I chuckled. "You almost met the ground too." Helping him into his North Face, I put on the matching hat, grabbed my wallet and keys, and we were out the door.

I walked into Sullivan & Co. with my future CEO at my side. I'd been working on building a legit cleaning empire over the last three years one contract at a time. My team consisted of ten women – sharp, organized, and they kept my business moving better than any Fortune 500 company. I'd handpicked all single mothers who were hustlers and as loyal as they come.

I made it my business to employ an all-female staff because the reality was, no one had the gift of gab like a woman. The way they finessed, contracts were as good as signed without negotiating our prices or standard of business.

"Morninggg," Kalia, the front desk receptionist, sang. "There go my favorite boy." Before she could get from behind the desk, EJ had run to her.

"You just love the ladies, don't you?" I said, grinning. "Good morning, Kalia. I have a visitor coming through at 12:30. Her name is Thyri Anderson. Can you make sure to escort her to my office when she gets here?"

"I sure can," she replied while tickling EJ. "You want me to take him to the kids' room?"

"Yes, please. Gimme five, man." I held my hand out for EJ to dap. He slapped it hard, and I pretended to be hurt. "Ahhh, man," I grabbed at my wrist, "you getting too strong for Daddy."

He smiled proudly, making me and Kalia laugh.

"That's cause he a big boy," Kalia added. "Come on, lemme get you set up."

"Oh," I stopped her, as she went to walk away, "how's Kayla?" I asked about her daughter.

"She's doing really good. My mom is home with her today. Thanks again for helping with the physical therapy, Enzo."

"No sweat. Glad she's on the mend. If you ever need her to

come here so you can keep an eye on her, I can have my cousin send someone over, and she can do her PT in the kids' room. This way you don't have to worry about her regressing."

She nodded. "I appreciate that and will keep it in mind." Smiling, she walked away to drop EJ off.

The kids' room was a space that I had specially designed for the children of my staff, so they never had to choose between work and childcare. With their input and even input from the kids through colorful sketches I had my designer come up with, we created an oasis for the kids to be kids. And I made sure to cover all basis from soft mats, toys for infants to toddlers, down to two flat screens and game systems set up for the pre-teens and teenagers. It was kind of like a home away from home that was fully monitored by two licensed care providers. Those providers also happened to be my cousins, Kyiris and Shawna. Keeping business in the family was my thing.

Heading into my office, I pulled out my phone to call my cousin, Aura. The phone rang a few times, and just as I was about to hang up, the call connected.

**"What's the word?"** he answered with a yawn.

**"Ain't no way you just now waking up, my nigga."** I glanced over at the clock, and it read 11:03 a.m.

**"Nah. I just got in the door like thirty minutes ago. Bout to shower and take my ass to sleep. Wassup?"**

**"You just getting back in town?"**

**"Yeah."**

**"Oh, aight. I ain't want shit, was just calling to tap in witchu."**

**"How'd the meeting go?"** he asked, and I knew he was referring to the hit.

**"Successful. Had an unexpected guest but nothing I couldn't handle."**

**"Oh. I know you went up by the hour."**

**"For sure."**

**"Copy. I don't hear your shadow in the background. He sleep?"**

"**Nah. We're at the office. I had some paperwork to handle, and I'm interviewing a potential nanny in a little bit.**"

He snickered before speaking. "**And who bout to watch his bad ass? Did you have to upload a tape of how he is on a daily basis?**"

I laughed. "**Nigga, fuck you. Y'all gon' stop talkin' bout my kid.**"

"**Mann,**" he chuckled, "**you know EJ my lil' potna, but that lil' nigga would give Super Nanny a run for her money.**"

"**Welp, let's hope shorty got what it takes.**" I shrugged.

"**Yeah. What's her name? I'ma pray for her before I go to sleep.**"

"**Nigga, pray for your sins. Get off my line.**"

"**Aight, what's her name forreal though?**"

"**Thyri.**"

"**Aight. I'ma pray that she fine, thick as hell, and can handle EJ.**"

"**I'm looking for a nanny, dawg. Not a date.**"

"**Nah, nigga, you looking for a helpmate too. You just don't know it. I'm bout to crash though. Love.**"

"**Love.**"

We ended the call, and I powered on the flat screen TV in front of my desk. The camera feed from the security monitors that I had around the property popped up on the screen. I zoomed in on the one that covered the parking lot. I wanted to see Thyri when she pulled up. Something about Aura's statement had me even more curious about her. Turning on my computer, I planned to busy myself with work until she arrived. This was going to be interesting.

## CHAPTER 4

# First Impressions & Afterthoughts

I fought the afternoon traffic in crowded ass New York City, determined to get to my interview on time. I knew I shouldn't have agreed to 12:30, but there was no turning back, and missing the interview was out of the question.

**"Alright, girl, I'm back,"** Danae announced, walking back into the camera in her uniform. She'd called while getting ready for the afternoon shift at the family-owned diner she managed. **"I need to hit the gym asap. These pants were not this damn tight two weeks ago."** Pulling at the waistline of her black pants, she shook her head.

**"Oh, please, girl. You just thick. And it looks good on you."**

**"I meannn, I never said I wasn't fine nie. I could lose a couple pounds though."**

I laughed at her cockiness, a trait we both shared.

**"Anyway, I called you this morning to get the rundown on what happened at the nursing home yesterday. Your text didn't tell me enough. I need the details."**

Exhaling hard, I gripped the steering wheel tight and gave her the play by play of the whole ordeal that almost had me in cuffs. By her wide eyes and the way she threw her head back, I knew the news had her as hot as me.

"Girl, get the fuck outta here. Why you ain't call me right then and there? One thing about it, you know I ain't scared to go to jail behind the people I love. Them bitches would've had to line it up. That's Poppa D. Are they crazy?!" she exclaimed.

My father was Danae's uncle on her mother's side, and they were close.

I almost laughed at her reaction because everything was always so animated with Danae. Ever since we were kids, whether she was recounting a story or listening, there was some type of dramatic movement in her response.

"Please, D. Even thinking about it now got me ready to lose it. But instead of wastin' my energy on them, I'm gonna put it into stacking my bread. I'm bringing my father home, and when I do, I wanna be sure he's equipped with everything he needs and then some. He needs top tier home care. And while I'm able to help him with some things, he needs professionals to aid in his recovery. I don't care what I gotta do to make it happen; it's gonna happen."

She hummed and nodded in agreement. "What you think about going back to work? Your supervisor said she'll always have a spot for you, remember?"

"I thought about it, but that field isn't for me anymore, D. Those emergency calls are still stuck with me today, and I can't handle it."

I was an EMT for two years when I met Kaleb, and I loved my job. Between the rush it gave me and the satisfaction of being a first responder, I never saw myself quitting. And then someone died on my shift. The whole scene messed me up bad. I'd done everything in my training to save the eight-year-old kid with a gunshot wound to the stomach, but we lost him. After seeing how it affected me weeks after, Kaleb and I made the mutual decision that it was best for me to quit. I found out I was pregnant with KJ weeks later, and the decision turned out to be for the best.

"I get it. So, what you gonna do?"

"Remember that night we were talking about jobs we'd wanna try out to see if we'd like it?"

"Yeah. I said stripper, and you said a nanny." She laughed. "We went to the club that night for research purposes, and I quickly surmised that I am no nasty dancer for money."

We both cracked up laughing. D had her face so scrunched up the entire night, you would've thought she smelled something foul.

"Bitch, you had a whole attitude."

"Yes, because I got to see firsthand just how cheap niggas were when it came to tipping the dancers. I make more with my regular salary at the diner. I was too through."

"Yeah, well, we know why you make more at the diner. What that man make you, like employee of the year?" I snickered.

"Of the month, heffa. And that's simply because a bitch be on her j... o... b. Not because the owner's brother wants something he can't have."

"Mmhmm. Well, it's my turn to do field research. I made a profile on Care.com, and I'm headed to my first interview."

"Well, damn. You could've given a better heads up, Thyri. I ain't even get to look into where you going. No address or nothing. You think you grown?" She playfully scolded with her hand on her hip.

"Just a lil' bit," I said, using my fingers to specify a little.

She laughed. "You right but still send it to me. People pose as something they ain't all the time. You don't really know who you meeting until you meet them."

"Which is the point, crazy girl. But I'm gonna tell you the address now. Write it down." I rambled the address off from my memory.

"Okay, got it. This should be interesting. Easy too if it's not a bad ass kid. Speaking of kids, how was pick up with KJ?"

"I'm meeting the kid today too. You know I love kids, so

I'm sure it'll be cool. As far as my kid, he's still not feeling me and didn't give me any more conversation other than a dry ass 'hey' when he got in the car and fake went to sleep."

She chuckled. "How you know he was faking?"

"Cause as soon as his phone rang, his eyes popped open to answer it. KJ is full of it."

"He still mad at you. He'll be aight. Christmas around the corner, so he want his gifts."

"Mmmhmm. Anywho, I just pulled up. Let me see where I can park at, so I'm not late."

"Okay. Good luck, boo. I'm at the diner til' seven tonight. Call me, beep me, if you wanna reach me."

"Bye, Nae Possible." Ending the call, I spotted a car pulling out of a spot and quickly reversed into it.

Double checking the address from the email, I nodded my approval. It wasn't the commercial building I expected to find. This was modern, sleek. The frosted glass doors had the name Sullivan & Co. Cleaning on it all sophisticated and shit. It gave luxury from the outside, so I could only imagine what the inside looked like.

Stepping out of the car, I looked down at my attire – a fitted, white, button up, collared shirt, black wide-legged pants, and a pair of Sambas on my feet. I wanted to be cute and comfortable. But after seeing the building, I felt like I was underdressed. I couldn't turn back now, so I continued forward.

Pulling the doors open, the lobby didn't disappoint. From the waterfall to the bright lighting and marble flooring, it didn't look like a cleaning business was run out of the place. It screamed 'money'.

"Welcome to Sullivan & Co. How can I help you?" A young woman seated behind an oversized desk greeted with a smile.

"Hi, my name is Thyri Anderson. I'm here to see..."

"Me."

I was cut off by a rough, but smooth, commanding voice that made the hairs on my neck stand up. The smile on the woman's face grew wider like she knew something I didn't. Or maybe her body had reacted the same way as mine at some point. I turned to find a fine ass man, about 6'4" in height. He was brown skinned with eyes that warned you. Whether the warning was good or not, I couldn't tell, but there was a warning. I took in the tattoos on his neck that were partially hidden by a crew neck sweater and scanned his whole body, stopping at the Timbs on his feet. Yeah, he was fine as fuck.

"Mr. Sullivan?" I asked for clarification, but I had a feeling that it was my potential employer.

"Enzo," he said, walking closer and holding his hand out for me to shake.

He didn't smile at first. He assessed. And not in a bad way. In a way that let me know he was observant. Like he saw everything at once. I placed my hand in his and immediately wanted to take it back. There was no reason my body was acting like I'd never touched the opposite sex before. It was like up close, he was even more fine and... present.

"I'll take it from here, Kalia." He spoke to the woman behind me with my hand still trapped in his. "Let's talk for a few then you can meet EJ. Cool?" he asked, finally releasing me.

"Sounds good."

"Good. Follow me."

I let him lead the way, following a few steps behind him, as I got a good look at the building. Sensing that I was lagging behind, he stopped mid walk and turned to me. I caught the silent 'walk up' in his look and smiled.

"I could walk a little faster, huh?" I joked, taking a couple steps forward so that I was at his side.

"You good," he replied.

Continuing forward, side by side, I felt so small next to him. I was 5'6", and he towered over my small frame. He opened the glass door to what looked like a conference room and let me enter first. I didn't know if it was the gentleman part or the way he looked down at me as I walked past him inside the room. Whatever it was, it had me secretly blushing hard.

Gesturing to a seat at the table, he sat down across from me and rested his arms lightly on the table.

"So," he started, "before we go into me asking whatever questions people ask in an interview, let me start by saying this is out of the norm for me. Not just seeking a nanny but the whole asking for help outside of my family. And even then, they gotta pull it out of me before I volunteer the ask." I caught a small, shy smile when he mentioned family. "Just a quick rundown, as you know, my name is Enzo. I own Sullivan & Co. Cleaning, which is obviously the building you're in now. I'm a single father of a two-year-old boy, Enzo Jr., who we call EJ. I'm seeking a nanny who values family and who can work around my schedule, which can get busy at times and things come up suddenly, but for the most part, I'm present. Most of all, I'm looking for someone who can keep up with my kid in my absence."

I digested his introduction, listening intently as he spoke, before responding. "Well, since you're being upfront, I'll follow suit. I have zero nanny experience. But I do have fifteen years parenting experience. I love kids. I have a medical background. I was an EMT for two years."

"What made you apply?" he asked.

I swallowed. "Other than it being something I know I can do, I need steady work that doesn't take me away from my father fully and has flexibility. My father is in a rehab facility recovering from a stroke, and I have a fifteen-year-old son who... let's just say I need to keep my eye on him. Flexibility is key."

He leaned back and nodded. "That's a lot to juggle."

His statement was true. It wasn't empathetic though. And I didn't take it in a bad way. It was more of an observation.

"As do you," I countered with my own observation. "Which is why you need a nanny, right?"

"That and because my family won't watch my bad ass son." He chuckled. "Their words, not mine."

I laughed along with him. "My dad used to say that about my son. He'd use rambunctious instead of bad though."

"Code word for bad as fuck."

"Pretty much."

We shared another laugh.

"How is EJ with new people?" I questioned. "Does he communicate? Well, as much as a two-year-old can I mean."

He chuckled. "Oh, yeah, he communicates. He's quiet for the first few minutes. I can tell when he don't vibe with a person because he won't leave my side. But if you good people, he can sense it. I know it probably sounds weird because he's only two, but kids are smart. They know when they not feeling someone."

"Oh, I absolutely agree. If you don't mind me asking, is his mom around?"

"Nah." He shook his head. "I'm a full-time single father."

I nodded. "That's... not easy."

"It has it's challenges, but for the most part, we straight."

Before I could speak again, there was a small knock at the door.

Enzo smiled and turned toward the door. "That might be your new client. Come in," he called out.

The door pushed open, and the cutest little boy bolted inside, running straight into Enzo's open arms.

"He had enough of the other kids. I think he needed a break." The woman from the front desk laughed.

"Thanks, Kalia."

"No problem." She closed the door, leaving me with Enzo and his mini.

"Hey, man. This is Ms. An..."

"Thyri." I cut him off. "He can call me Thyri. Hi, handsome." I spoke to EJ, whose face lit up like he'd seen me before. He then leaned forward on the table and held his hand out to me. "Oh," I said, getting up with my hand out.

He went to put his leg up like he was going to climb up on the table, only to be stopped by Enzo's voice.

"We ain't doing that. Here." He sat him down on his feet. "Go around and shake her hand."

"I'll meet you halfway," I compromised.

We walked around the table at the same time, and I kneeled

down to shake his hand. My heart melted when he put his little hand in mine. It made me think about KJ at his age. EJ's chubby, dimpled cheeks, his big brown eyes, and Timbs on to match his daddy's was just too cute.

"Hi," he said clearly.

"Hi, handsome. Nice to meet you."

He looked back to Enzo, whose eyes flickered to mine, and smiled. That subtle look alone had my stomach doing shit it wasn't supposed to be doing.

"Nice me you. EJ." He pointed to himself.

"Yes. Your name is EJ. I like your twists." I pointed out.

"My hair." He touched his head, making Enzo laugh.

"I forgot to tell you he was a parrot too."

I smirked and stood up straight. Enzo motioned with his head for him to go back to his side.

"That's cool. It shows his understanding. He's adorable."

Enzo's eyes softened noticeably. The pride of being a father was written all over his face. "Thank you. He's a handful. He think he grown too, but he's a dope kid. If it's something you think you can handle, I'd like to move forward."

"Yes, of course. Is there anything else you need from me other than what may already be in my Care.com profile?"

"Yeah. Your permission for me to do my own background check."

I paused, processing his request. I mean, it wasn't unreasonable seeing as I was a stranger who would be taking care of his child in his home. I just didn't think someone would be so upfront with the request.

"That's fair," I responded with my approval. "Is there anything I need to provide?" I questioned. "It's not every day that one asks to do a background check on me."

"I like to take precautions. And nah, I don't need anything. Once I get the results back, I'll shoot you an email with the pay rate, and then we can schedule a day for you to come by and maybe shadow me for a few hours to see his routine."

"Okay," I said, grabbing my purse. "Well, thank you again for having me. It was nice meeting you both. Bye, EJ."

"Bye, Tyri," he let out, putting his own spin on my name.

"Yep, that's me," I replied with a smile, not bothering to correct him.

"We'll walk you out," Enzo suggested before walking over and opening the door. EJ stood up against it, helping to hold it open.

"Thank you so much," I said to him.

He gave me another big smile that warmed my heart. EJ walked between the two of us, as we made our way to the front. I waved bye to the receptionist, who returned the wave along with a nod. Stepping out into the cold air, something prompted me to take one last glance through the frosted glass. I caught Enzo watching me walk away. It wasn't weird or in a way that would suggest that he was lusting after me. Just... noticing.

And something in the way he noticed me made me hope that the background check results came back sooner than later. I was ready to start my new job for more than one reason now. Super Nanny who? The fine nanny was on deck.

CHAPTER 5

# The Nanny's First Day

When I asked Thyri her permission to run a background check, it was a test to see if she was hiding anything or came with bullshit. Her 'yes' wasn't immediate, but I understood the reason behind her hesitance. However, the background check was happening whether she agreed to it or not. Her willingness gave her a one up in my book. I didn't allow people in my space without knowing who they were, who they were connected to, and who they came from.

I took no one at face value and didn't make moves on vibes or anyone's words alone. You had to show more than tell. And here I was, two days after our initial meeting, going through the files my aunt sent to my email. At fifty-six years old, my Aunty Juanita was the Sullivan family's go to when we needed information. She was a beast on the computer and could get in anywhere we needed her.

I had two files containing all things Thyri Anderson. Aunt Juanita had run a standard background check first that included her criminal, employment, and credit history. Everything was clean. She didn't have so much as a speeding ticket on record. A real law-abiding citizen.

And then we dug deeper, searching the people closest to her, immediate family and associates included. I confirmed that she did have a teenage son and a father who was in a rehabilitation center. A mother and sister who lived out of state and an ex-husband who still contributed from behind the wall. At least that was what the first of the month transfers into her account labeled monthly bills stated. Of course, I looked into his charges then did a street analysis on him. Nothing came back that I was concerned about. I didn't want to scare her off, so the extent of the background check that included her family, I'd keep to myself.

Having carefully thumbed through the files, I was ready to move forward, so I opened up a new draft to send her an email.

To: Thyri.Anderson@gmail.com

Good afternoon, Thyri,

I hope this message finds you well. I wanted to reach out to let you know that your background check came back clean. If you're still interested in the position, feel free to give me a call at your convenience. My cell number is 917-364-4140.

I read the email over after hitting send and wished I'd gone over it beforehand. That whole 'I hope this message finds you well' shit sounded so corny. The cost of being professional.

My phone rang minutes later on my desk with an incoming call from an unsaved number. I rarely gave out my personal number. Figuring it was Thyri, I answered on the third ring.

**"Hello?"**

**"Hey, Enzo. It's Thyri."** Her voice was upbeat.

**"Wassup, Thyri? How's your day going?"** I asked casually.

There was a brief pause. I could hear movement in the background, followed by a clinking noise.

**"Give me one second,"** she said before the phone went silent. After a few seconds, her voice came through again. **"Sorry about that. I was fighting for my life trying to hang this garland. I got your email. Thanks for the update. As far as the position, I'm ready when you are."**

**"Cool. I know you mentioned only being available on alternate weekends. With today being Saturday, would you be available to come by the house for a few hours? You can see EJ in his element and see how we run our day to day."**

"Sure. My son left me for the weekend, and I checked on my father, so I'm free."

"Sounds good. I'm gonna shoot the address to you via text, and I'll see you in a few."

"Perfect. Thanks again for the opportunity."

"You're welcome."

She hung up first, and I sent the address over. Shutting my computer down, I walked out of my office and down the hall to Enzo's room. We'd just finished having a breakfast of champions and morning conversation. Pushing his room door open, I found him trying to pull the sheets off his bed.

"What happened, dawg?" I asked the question but kinda knew the answer from the small pair of Hanes boxers on the floor next to the bed.

"I pee, Daddy. I sorry."

I smiled. "You good, man. Accidents happen. But I can't have you wit' your Johnson all out. Come get in the tub, and Daddy will change the sheets, aight?"

"Okayy," he dragged out with his head down.

"Head up, EJ. Daddy not mad. Come here." He walked over to me, covering himself with his small hands. "Hold your head up." He lifted his head. "Were you holding your pee?"

"I hold it."

"Don't do that no more, aight? When you gotta go, go. Big boys don't pee on they self."

"Okay."

"Aight. Come on."

Ushering him to the bathroom, I helped him wash up and change. He was well on his way to being fully potty trained, only wearing pull ups at night. Even then, I made sure to take him to the bathroom whenever I got up. I couldn't have my boy being labeled as anyone's piss pot, so potty training before three was a must. After tossing the sheets sand blanket into the wash, he helped me put on fresh linen.

As I chilled with him in his room, I remembered that I hadn't

43

given Thyri a time to come through. Pulling my phone from my basketball shorts, I sent her a text.

Me: I just noticed I hadn't given you a time to come by. Does two o'clock work for you?

347-497-8437: It does. I meant to ask you the other day, is EJ potty trained?

Me: He's at about 85%. We plan to be fully potty trained before January 1st.

347-497-8437: We'll make it happen. See you soon.

Reading her text, I looked over at EJ, who sat in his recliner with his hand behind his head. I'd secured a nanny. Now, I had to sit back and watch things play out.

---

THYRI PULLED up to the house a few minutes before two. I stood at the front window, watching her pull a white Range into my driveway. Yonkers was quieter than the city. I lived in a ducked off neighborhood where people pretty much stayed to themselves. It was one of the reasons I'd chose it out of the four houses my cousin, Minnie, had me tour. It was private and spacious, more house than me and EJ needed but the perfect fit, nonetheless.

I watched as she stepped out of her car, swinging her purse over her shoulder and glancing behind her before proceeding to the front door. She was aware. Alert. Her movement seemed like it was second nature to her, like something she'd learned growing up. I made mental note about it. Being alert was an important part of her job.

Walking over to the door, I opened it before she could knock.

"Reporting for duty." She smiled.

"Come in," I said, gesturing with my head for her to come inside. "I can take your coat."

"Thank you." Pulling her full length coat off, she handed it to me.

As I walked around her to hang her coat up, I caught a glimpse of her ass. That mothafucka was shaped like the ripest peach. I wasn't sure what I expected for her nanny attire, but if this yoga set she had on was the standard, I was wit' it. Yeah, I had told Aura I wasn't looking for a date, and I really wasn't on the market for a woman. A nigga had eyes though. And I hoped that she had this set in every color.

"It's really cozy in here. And it smells good. You sure there's no woman living here?" She turned to me with her hand on her hip.

I chuckled. "Why a woman gotta live here for a nigga shit to be clean and smell good? How you know I don't take the trips to Burlington Maxx and At Home for the smell good shit and cozy shit?"

She covered her mouth to stifle a giggle. "I would've believed you had you not combined the names of two stores. It's Burlington and TJ Maxx."

"Oh," I replied, caught. "I mean, I do shit. For the most part, when my moms see something that fits the house, she just picks it up, drops it off to me, and I make it work."

"You're doing a good job," she complimented.

"Thank you."

"If you don't mind, I brought some shoes to change into. I didn't want to track snow all on your floor, and I don't wanna walk around barefoot."

"That's cool. You can change, and I'll put your boots in the laundry room. EJ just went down for a nap not too long ago, so I'll give you a quick tour."

"Naps are essential so good for him."

Once she was changed into a pair of bedazzled Crocs, I gave her the tour. We started in the laundry room, then the living room, kitchen, dining room, EJ's playroom, the two guest bedrooms, and guest bathrooms. I left EJ's room for last, wanting him to show her around once he was up.

"This is a kid's playground," she commented, as I closed the door to the playroom.

"Yeah. I think all the options overstimulate him sometimes. That's why he's usually in his room or my room, flipping on some shit."

She laughed, following me into the kitchen where we sat at the island to talk the numbers and duties. She was direct with her expectations. Asked questions that mattered. Repeated numbers back to me for clarification and basically negotiated her own salary with no objection from me. We also discussed ways to go about caring for EJ. I was clear on what worked, and she gave her insight from a mom standpoint.

"Kids thrive when there's consistency and a schedule in place." She pointed out after I mentioned that EJ didn't really have a set schedule or a bedtime.

"So, I shouldn't let him tire himself out by bouncing off the wall?"

"I'm not necessarily saying that. But if he had a schedule he ran off of, it wouldn't take bouncing off the walls for him to be tired. And I know schedule sounds so formal, but there's ways to make that fun. Same when it comes to potty training."

I nodded slowly, stroking my goatee. "I see. Well, you're the new sheriff on the block. I'm open to see your way of doing things."

"I'm not the new sheriff. We're a team. Team EJ," she said proudly with her fist out.

"Team EJ don't do no corny ass fists bumping." I held out my open hand, and she giggled, placing hers in mine. "We shake on it." Her hand was so soft, I almost didn't want to let it go. I thought she knew it too because she didn't pull away immediately after the shake.

"You mind if I cook something for dinner?" She glanced toward the stove. "I can whip him up a quick snack for when he wakes up too."

I raised a brow. "You sure? I didn't expect to have you in the kitchen on your first day. But if you insist, do ya thang."

"I don't mind at all. I love to cook. What's his favorite meal?"

"Oatmeal. But he don't fuck wit' nobody oatmeal but my mama's. I won't even tell you what he did to me when I tried to make him some."

She stood from the island. "I'm up for the challenge. Any dinner requests? I mean, you gotta eat too, so you can give me something you both like for that."

"Steak bites, mashed potatoes, and spinach."

"Dang, you must've been thinkin' bout that since last night," she joked.

"I have."

"Okay. Give me a tour of your cabinets and fridge, and I'm on it."

It was a good thing that we were fully stocked with everything she needed because she was able to get started right away. I sat back, watching her wash her hands before moving about the kitchen like the house was her second home. She was polite, asking before she took out a pot or reached for something we hadn't already set out.

We talked while she cooked, getting to know each other. The conversation flowed effortlessly. It wasn't forced with meaningless words just to fill the silence. Thyri told me about her son being a star player on his high school basketball team with the potential of being in the league someday. I could tell she was proud of him.

"You have vanilla extract?" she asked while stirring the oatmeal on the stove.

"Cabinet on your right. What's your backup plan if he don't like it?" I questioned, as she mixed in a few drops of the vanilla extract.

She turned slightly with a smirk. "You hating already on my first full day?"

"Hey," I said with my hands up. "I'm just saying EJ will spit that shit out if he not fucking wit' it. He did it to me, and I ain't looked at oatmeal the same since." I shook my head, thinking back to the surgical clean up I had to do.

Laughing, she turned the stove off. "I don't need a backup plan, Enzo. I got this. Trust me."

Her laughter did something to the room. The only way I could explain it was the feeling of a void being filled, oddly enough. Hearing my phone ring from the living room, I got up to answer it. Seeing Aura's name on the caller ID, I took the call in my room.

"**What's good?**" I spoke, closing the door behind me.

"**Work,**" **he replied.** "**You busy?**"

"**How long is the job?**"

"**Are you busy?**" he repeated.

"**Does it matter? You called for a reason. How long is the job?**"

"**A few hours. Meet at the diner in an hour to go over details.**"

"**Copy.**"

Ending the call, I grabbed my personal phone to call my mother. I knew she was gon' get on my ass about the last minute call, but I needed her.

"Daddy," I heard EJ call out to me.

"Here I come, E."

After a few rings, her phone went to voicemail. I called again, placing the phone on speaker, as I changed into a pair of black jeans, black hoodie, and pulled a pair of field boots out the closet. Again, the phone went to voicemail. This time, I left a message for her to call me back.

"Daddyyy!" EJ yelled out again impatiently.

Walking out of my room, I met Thyri making her way down the hall.

"May I?" she asked, stopping in front of EJ's door.

"Go head."

She pushed the door open, and EJ's head whipped in our direction.

"Hey, EJ," she greeted.

"Hi, Tyri." He smiled, showing his small teeth.

He remembered her name. That meant something.

"I hungry." He rubbed his stomach, making Thyri laugh.

"Her name is Thyri, EJ. Thyri is your new nanny. She's gonna watch you when Daddy not home."

"I made you oatmeal," she said. "You wanna try it out?"

"Yes!" he replied, excited.

"Okay, come on." She held her hand out to him, and he went to her without hesitation.

I watched from the entryway, as she propped him up in his booster seat at the island and placed a bowl in front of him. I silently prayed that he didn't vomit. Leaning over the island, she handed him the spoon and a napkin while grinning.

"EJ," she spoke in a soft tone, "if you don't like, you can spit it out in this napkin, okay?"

Examining the oatmeal, he nodded feverishly.

Thyri glanced up at me, flashing a quick smile, and crossed her fingers. EJ ate a spoonful, twisted his mouth as he chewed, then took another. We both looked on in silence, me wondering how she'd cracked the oatmeal code and Thyri basking in her first win on her first day.

"It's good, huh?" She pushed further for confirmation.

EJ gave her a thumbs up and a head nod.

"Looks like Grandma got competition."

"Nah." She giggled. "Not competition. Teamwork makes the dream work, remember?"

I smirked and nodded. "That's what they say. But I gotta make a quick run. Something came up. I'm waiting on the call back from Moms, so she can come and hold him down, while I'm gone."

"Oh, okay. I can stay until you get back. I can work on dinner, hang with EJ, and put him to bed if you're back too late."

"You sure?"

I studied her face, and she flashed a genuine, confident smile. "Positive. My son isn't home, so EJ will really be keeping me company. If you still wanna have your mom come, that's fine too."

"Aight. That'll work. If I'm out too long, I'll give you a call."

"Sounds good."

Walking over to EJ, I ruffled his head. "Daddy be back, aight? You're gonna stay with Thyri."

"Okay. I finish, Daddy. More please." He held up his empty bowl, and Thryi took it from him.

"I got you. Tell Daddy we got this, EJ. We bout to have some fun."

"We have fun, Daddy."

"Save some fun for me too, man. Oh, and Thyri, the code to the alarm is 0627. I'm gonna arm it when I leave out."

She nodded. "Got it."

Confident that EJ was in good hands, I grabbed my coat and headed for the door.

"Hey," she called out, peeking around the corner.

"Wassup?"

"Is he allergic to anything?"

"Nah. He straight."

"Okay, cool. We'll be here when you get back. Be safe."

The last part of her statement hung in the air and followed me to my car. The thought of a woman waiting at home for me with my son had never crossed my mind... until now.

## CHAPTER 6
# A Moment Held

Me: You ready to quit yet?

Thyri: Lol. Why would I be ready to do that?

Me: Cause I know my son bad as hell. That's
why my mama don't wanna watch him no
more. She say he wear her edges thin. 😅

Thyri: 😅😅😅 well, he's been good with me.
We read two books, played blocks, and now
we're just talking. He's doing most of the
talking though, and I'm just trying my best to
put everything together. I think I'm doing a
good job, by the way.

Me: Lmao. Oh, he puttin' on a show.

Thyri: Well, I did set the rules up front. We
haven't had any issues… yet. If he get to
cuttin' up, I'll make sure I'm outside of the
cameras.

Me: They won't find your body 😊. I'll let you
get back to your duties.

I texted Thyri's phone after a few hours to check in on EJ, and it seemed that they were getting along well. My mother had returned my call, letting me know she wouldn't be able to make it. When I told her that Thyri had it handled, she was shocked that I'd left her alone on her first day. Once she was over the shock of it all, she commended me for stepping out of my comfort zone. It was a big step too.

"So, what you think we should tell the family?" Aura asked, staring straight ahead.

We were parked outside of an industrial building in Long Island. What I thought was going to be a quick in and out hit turned out to be a meeting/interrogation to determine if a hit was necessary. It was a sensitive matter that Aura could've handled solo, but he needed a second opinion. Someone under the Sullivan umbrella had attempted to go rogue right under our noses with hopes that they could fly under the radar while doing so. We valued family, both close and distant. So, to have one of our own go against the grain was a hard pill to swallow. Having to put them down because of it was too... at least it was for Aura.

"You don't have to tell the family shit. The only person you owe an explanation is your sister. It's her nigga laying in there with his brain matter on the ground."

"I really don't owe her shit either. I might yoke her ass up for even bringing this nigga in my presence. How you gon' try to do your own shit under my shit?"

"I can't answer that question for you. I don't partake in ho ass nigga thoughts." My phone chimed in my lap. It was a text from two of my cleaners. "The girls are pulling up now. I trust that they'll have everything done in two hours at the most. They'll wrap the body, but you gotta do the disposal."

"Why you telling me like you not gon' be here to see to it that they do?"

"Cause I'm not. I don't do clean up. I put the bullets in niggas." Stepping out his car, I paused. "Besides, I gotta get back to the crib. I got a nanny I gotta relieve, remember?"

"Forgot all about that shit. Aight, cool. Yo, don't forget we're doing that Secret Santa shit this year for the Christmas party. And don't act like you don't know nothing bout it, nigga. Kyiris said she went to your house and had you pick your person."

I chuckled at him calling me out before I could lie. "And you know what's crazy? I picked her ass. I can't wait to get her some shit from the Dollar General just for putting my business out there."

He laughed, slapping his hands together. "Do it. You know how that girl feel about Christmas. She might spazz on yo' ass. But the party is at the diner this year. I paid to have it all decked out."

"Aight, cool. Hit me if you need me before then. Love."

"Love."

I hopped back in my car and made the hour and a half trip back home. I thought about calling Thyri to let her know that I was en route but decided against it. I didn't want her to think that I was monitoring her. As I drove with Meek Mills' latest EP playing low, my phone rang in the center console. Thinking it was Thyri calling, I reached for it. It wasn't Thyri. The words Private Caller danced across the screen, and I let the call go to voicemail.

I thought for sure that the person on the other end had the wrong number, but the phone rang again a few minutes later. This time, I answered.

**"Fuck is this?"** My greeting was anything but pleasant.

**"Hey, Enzo."** The voice on the other end came through, and I could feel the anger building up inside of me that I tried to suppress daily. **"You there?"**

**"Why you callin' me, Kennedy?"** I asked EJ's egg donor whose voice I hadn't heard in two years but could make out in a room full of people.

**"How you been?"** She acted like we were old friends from high school who happened to bump into each other in the mall.

Crazy to me because the last I checked, we were parents of a child she abandoned.

**"Kennedy, don't make me disrespect you. State your business."**

There was an awkward silence before she responded. **"I wa...
Listen, I didn't call to fight with you or tie your line up. I'm
calling about EJ. How is he doing?"**

"Did it hurt, Kennedy?"

"What? Did what hurt?"

"When you bumped your fuckin' head before dialing my
number. Or maybe somebody pushed you to do it. Cause
you ain't checked on my son in two years."

Hearing her sigh heavily, I found myself getting even more
pissed off.

**"I'm calling because my husband thought it would be
nice if EJ spent Christmas Eve with us. We're doing a
holiday photoshoot with our son and our parents. It'll be a
great time for him to meet his little brother and the rest of
the family."**

I laughed, but the tone of my laughter was humorless. **"It
gotta be coke,"** I let out. **"Let me make sure I'm hearing you
correctly. This was your husband's idea to reach out to your
son for the holidays? Cause fuck his birthday that was a few
months ago, huh? My bad, the last two birthdays."**

**"Enzo..."**

**"Nah,"** I cut her off. **"You and yo' family not bout to use
MY fuckin' son as a photo op, so y'all can portray the
perfect family. Your nigga clearly don't know who the fuck
I am, but it would do you well to educate him."**

**"That's not fair, Enzo,"** she said weakly. **"I'm his mother. I
have just as much right to Enzo Jr. as you do."**

**"You left your rights at the hospital on September 8th,
2023. Elephants, grizzly bears, cheetahs, wolf spiders,
dolphins, and honey badgers are mothers. You, Kennedy, are
an egg donor. You gotta know the difference."**

**"I'm just try..."**

**"That's the shit I'm talking' bout! You don't get to 'try'
at your convenience. You don't get to 'try' at EJ's expense."** I
couldn't believe that I was on the phone that I paid for arguing
with this silly ho. This shit wasn't P at all.

**"At my convenience? How about you can't string a woman on for two years, making her think you were building something, and then decide we're not at your convenience! You abandoned me, Enzo,"** she cried out.

**"And you abandoned my son. Only difference is, I'll be around to wipe his tears when he realizes it. I could give a fuck about yours. Fuck off my phone."** Ending the call, I picked up my phone to block her number. She had me .38 hot.

I hoped that it was the last I heard from Kennedy. If she knew like I knew, she'd play in traffic before playing with me about EJ. After tonight, it seemed like I might have to remind her of that.

---

I pulled into my driveway, jaw tight, my mind replaying the conversation with Kennedy – if I could even call it that. The anger I felt wasn't just because she abandoned EJ, but also because she felt that another child deserved her presence more than her first born, like my boy wasn't good enough to stay. Some shit was just unforgiveable. This was one of those things.

Entering the house, I expected it to be quiet due to how late it was. What I didn't expect was the peace that came over me once I came in. It was like my anger had dissipated, and my jawline relaxed immediately. The silence was different. Settled. Almost as if it had been awaiting my arrival to partake in the stillness.

Taking my boots and coat off at the door, I walked farther into the house and froze at the sight before me. Thyri sat upright, asleep with her read rested on the cushion. On her lap, EJ lay stretched out, fast asleep, with his mouth slightly open. Her hand rested on his back protectively, as if this were how they normally slept. It was a Kodak moment, only it would have been odd for me to snap a picture of my son asleep with his new nanny.

As I stood there, watching, the contrast of what Kennedy refused to give my son versus what a stranger was willing to offer blew my fucking mind. Moving carefully, I went to lift EJ from her lap, and her eyes popped open – alert and protective.

"It's me. Y'all good," I said gently, my words matching her demeanor.

The recognition set in, as she blinked slowly. "Oh, shit," she whispered. "I'm sorry. I didn't mean to fall asleep." Still holding onto EJ, she sat up straight.

"You good. Let me put him in bed real quick." Careful not to wake him, I lifted EJ from her lap.

"Okay."

EJ's room was cleaner than I'd left it earlier. The toy cars and wrestling figures that littered the floor were put away, and his mini library was organized by book size. I nodded my appreciation while tucking him in. Pulling the comforter over his little body, I dimmed the light and headed back out front.

Back in the living room, I caught Thyri mid-stretch. The sweater she had on lifted just enough to expose her small back. Shit looked soft as hell. I could see the remnants of stretch marks that had faded away over time on her brown skin. It was sexy, real woman shit that I admired. Not in a lust filled, "I wanna fuck you" kinda way but in appreciation of her motherhood.

Dropping her hands, she turned slowly, and we locked eyes. She tilted her head to the side a little, and her mouth formed a sly grin, like she'd caught me staring.

"Everything okay?"

"Yeah. Preciate you holding it down. I see what you did in the room too. Thank you."

"Oh," she smiled, "you mean what **we** did in the room? He gave me a little pushback about cleaning at first, but I turned clean up time into a game, and he got on board. The only other competitive two-year-old I've ever encountered is my son when he was that age. Anything he didn't want to do or gave me a hard time about, I made it into a game. Worked like a charm."

"That's another thing I may be responsible for. We're both competitive. Unlike some parents, I don't let him win everything because of his size or his age. Ain't no pity wins over here. We're building character. Training him to be solid."

"Love that for him. Kids need that, especially boys. Oh, and dinner was a hit, just like the oatmeal." She patted herself on the back. "I put the leftovers away. Umm, I didn't give him a shower. Didn't know how you felt about that just yet. We did brush his teeth though."

I nodded. "I respect that. I'm cool with it so long as he is."

She checked the time on her watch and yawned. "Welp, it's late, and I think my job is done here for tonight. I'm gonna head…"

"No," I said. "You're staying the night."

"Who?" she questioned with a raised brow.

"You," I confirmed, not knowing where the sudden urge to want to keep her around came from.

"Umm, I know today was successful and all, but you do know you can't hold me hostage, right?"

I chuckled lowly. "I ain't tryna hold you hostage, shorty. It's late, and there's a snowstorm headed our way."

"Damn, really?"

"Yeah."

"I can get a hotel for the night." She hesitated. "I don't think it's appropriate for me to spend the night, Enzo."

"I wasn't asking you to stay, Thyri. I'm insisting. I'll pull both of our cars into the garage. Make sure you check in on KJ."

I left her in the living room and walked off to the back to reset the guest bedroom. *Did I just force my nanny to spend the night?* I thought. I didn't know what came over me. All I knew was I couldn't unring the bell. Didn't want to. Fuck it.

I went to pull the sheets off the bed when my phone rang in my pocket. Pulling it out, Aura's name flashed on the screen. He was the one person you didn't want to talk to after having made a split decision that was out of character. I knew this nigga would give me hell. And for a minute, I started to ignore the call but said fuck it. I was a grown ass man. I didn't have to explain shit to nobody. Besides, if Thyri was on fuck shit, I'd put a hole in her pretty little forehead.

**"What's good, nigga?"**

"I meant to tell you this shit earlier. I put my ear to the streets to see if your nanny was in 'em."

Laughing, I shook my head. "I'm not surprised. You know I handled that myself, right?"

"Yeah. I know you just as thorough as me. But what's better than two eyes? Four, right?"

"Can't argue witchu there. What you find out?"

"She was married to a nigga named Kaleb. He got a brother named Koric. Solid dudes. Kaleb used to have some shit going on in The Bronx. But his bread and butter was out in Georgia. He moved there and got shit popping on the scam and money laundering tip. His brother, Koric. is still up this way doing his one, two. Nothing major. From the looks of it, shorty was put up for a time."

"That's more to add to what I know thus far. Good looking out."

"You know how I'm coming bout the family. How she do with EJ alone?"

"Better than expected. She cracked the oatmeal code. Had his lil' ass in here cleaning and shit. A good hire."

"Oh, yeah. You know it get critical bout that oatmeal. That's wassup. She coming back in the morning?"

I went silent. This nigga was fishing for info like he knew something already and was waiting for me to confirm.

"Yeah. She'll be here. She's staying the night."

"Wordddd?"

His response was different than what I expected.

"Yeah. And ion wanna hear shit about it."

"Shiiiddd, mothafuckas out here marrying people they meet for the first time on some social experiment type shit. If you want yo' nanny to spend the night, YOLO."

"You been watching TV with Grandma Lettie again." I snickered.

"Man, I'ma bout to stop popping up on that old lady. The other day, she had me stuck on this *Love At First Sight* shit. I'm like mannn, ain't no fuckin' way."

"She gon' put an APB out on your ass, you stop coming by."

"You right. She might think something happened to her favorite grandson. But anyway, rock out, my nigga. Life's too short... bust yo' nanny down today. You done inspired me to go out on a limb my damn self now."

"Get off my phone, dawg."

"Aight. I'ma go. Love, nigga."

"Love."

Ending the call, I put the fresh linens on the bed before going to check on Thyri. As I walked back out into the living room, I could hear her talking on the phone.

"I called yo' ass for some advice that made sense, and you over here encouraging me to stay the night at this man house." I heard Thyri whispering. Well, at least she was trying to.

She paused, I assumed, to let the person on the other end talk before speaking again. "Of course I don't wanna drive in the snow, and I am comfortable, but what if this man tries to fuck me, Danae? Hold on, my headphones dying."

"If he tries to fuck you, then you fuck back." I heard the other person say.

"Oh, shit. You were on speaker." She fumbled with the phone, and I felt it was the best time to make my presence known.

"You straight?" I asked.

She turned around quickly with wide eyes. "I'ma call you back, D." Ending the call, she held her phone up to her head with her eyes closed. "I would hate to know how much of that conversation you actually heard."

"I heard the part about you not wanting to drive in the snow and the part about you fuckin' back."

"Yeah, lemme go home."

"You good, girl. My word. A nigga ain't hard up for no pussy. It's a safety thing for me. And by the way you were sleeping, I can tell you're tired. Stay here tonight and we'll see how things look in the morning. Cool?"

She folded her arms across her chest and squinted. "You want some company, Enzo?"

I laughed her off. "Come on, lemme show you where you'll be sleeping."

"I can't believe I'm doing this," she murmured, picking up her bag from the couch and walking toward me. "You sure about this?"

"I left you in my house alone for hours with the most important person in my life. If I was sure about that decision, I'm positive about this one. I'll take your key, so I can move your car."

Although still skeptical, she dug into her purse and placed her keys in my hand.

"Follow me."

I walked her down the hall and into the guest bedroom. Taking her into the bathroom, I pointed out the fresh towels and washcloths, offering to give her something to sleep in if she wanted to shower. She respectfully declined, and I didn't push for obvious reasons.

"You need anything? Charger for your phone? More pillows?"

"No," she said, looking around the room. "This is fine."

"Okay, cool. I'ma go move the cars and get settled in."

"Alright," she let out softly.

We stood there, staring at each other, likely trying to figure out what exactly was going on here.

"Good night, Enzo," she finally spoke.

"Good night, shorty."

Leaving out of the room, I closed the door behind me. I didn't know how I'd feel in the morning about my decision. All I knew was I didn't want to part with the peace that came with Thyri's presence tonight.

CHAPTER 7

# A Helping Hand Indeed

"How did a day job suddenly turn into an overnight stay?" I said out loud, in disbelief that I actually agreed to stay the night at Enzo's house.

I sat on the edge of the bed in his guest bedroom long after he'd left the room, just staring at my bag that sat on a chair across from the bed. Everything in me said to grab my bag and take my chances with the impending storm, but I knew it'd be just my luck that on my way home, the snow would hit, and I'd somehow be stuck out there. Still, a sleepover wasn't in the cards. I turned my head slightly toward the closed door. This shit was really happening.

What was worse than me making the decision was that I was comfortable – my body was at least. My mind... that was running in overdrive, making up different scenarios. But my body was settled. The set up of the room may have had something to do with that too. It smelled clean and was just as cozy as the rest of the house. Somehow, that made my mind more uneasy than if the room had been disorganized and funky. Because why did I feel so goddamn comfortable?

Running my hands over my thighs, I exhaled in an effort to ease my mind. Kicking my Crocs off, I sat on the bed Indian style and reached for my phone. Danae's voice popped in my head before I unlocked it.

*"Girl, stay the night. That man ain't gon' harm you. I think it's cute he's considering your safety." "If he try to fuck you, then you fuck back."*

Scrolling to our text thread, I typed fast.

> Me: I just wanna let you know that you're a terrible influence. And he heard you talkin' about fuckin', nasty ass.

Her reply came instant, like she was by the phone, waiting for an update.

> Danae: I'm glad he did hear me because I said what I said. A lil' one night stand ain't never hurt nobody. Add in a lil' hunching in the workplace and I'm here for it.

> Me: Is there something you wanna confess about your work husband? Cause I'm all ears.

I smiled while typing, knowing my text would get her riled up.

> Danae: That is not my work husband. Just a nigga who won't take no for an answer. Don't matter how many languages I say it in.

> Me: Yeah, okay. I'm gonna try to get some sleep in this house that doesn't belong to me.

> Danae: 😴😴 sleep tight. Don't let the fine man bite.

I rolled my eyes, smiling despite the situation, and exited our thread. Laying back on the bed, I welcomed the silence of the house. Staring at the ceiling, I thought about the day I had with EJ. His burst of energy left no room for me to sit down. He was so sweet and listened intently. I didn't see the bad side Enzo referred to. He just needed to learn how to manage all of that energy. And that was something I started with him today.

The way he listened, how he watched me when I moved, and the way he nodded like he understood more than he could say reminded me of KJ at that age. It was a testament to Enzo's parenting. He talked to EJ like he mattered. Like his voice, although small and sometimes incoherent, mattered. A real father.

Turning onto my side where I got the most comfortable sleep, I pulled the comforter over my body. Before closing my eyes, I sent my last text, this time to the most important person in my life.

<blockquote>Me: I'll be by Danae's house tomorrow night to pick you up. I love you.</blockquote>

The three dots appeared, and I held in a breath, hoping that he responded. I loved my son, and I hated when he shut me out. Just as I was preparing for the worst, his response came through.

<blockquote>Sonshine: I love you too.</blockquote>

That response worked for me. Setting my phone on the pillow next to me, I closed my eyes and drifted into an easy sleep.

The sudden urge to pee hit me in the middle of the night, waking me from a deep slumber. Getting up from the bed, I pushed myself forward to empty my bladder. My throat was dry, so after washing my hands, I left out of the room to grab a bottled water from the fridge. The lights from their Christmas tree guided me out to the front, where I could hear the rustling of paper. I spotted Enzo standing in the middle of the living room, shirtless, in a pair of plaid pajama pants that hung off his waist, showing the hem of his boxers.

The way the lights from the tree and the fireplace illuminated on his skin, I lowkey felt a little drool slip from my mouth that slurped back up real fast. He was sexy as fuck. The tattoos and the eight pack he possessed did something to my body. I continued forward, swallowing hard once he looked up at me.

"You look like you could use a hand," I spoke first, glancing down at a few poorly wrapped gifts and a stack of toys behind him that were up next for the same ill treatment.

He chuckled. "What gave it away? The partially wrapped guitar or the toolset where I used a little too much wrapping paper?"

"All of it." I burst out laughing. "This is horrible. You can't do my boy like this."

"Mann, you just met that kid," he teased.

"Yep, and we already got a secret handshake. Now what?" I rolled my neck and stuck my tongue out at him.

"Oh, word? Yeah, you're official."

"This I know. Now, come on. I'ma bout to give you wrapping 101. I hope you got more paper because we gon' start with unwrapping the few things you botched and then start over."

"Listen, I'm good at a lot of things. This right here ain't my strong suit."

"At all," I agreed, giggling. "Grab me a bottle of water and we gon' get to work."

I found a spot on the floor and began to rip the paper off the gifts he'd already wrapped. Once he was back with the water, I handed him something small to start with and set a box the same size in front of me. Taking him step by step through the process, he was able to wrap the box perfectly on the first try.

"If only more men could take that kind of direction, things would be alright with the world," I reasoned while taking a sip of my water.

"You think men don't listen?" he questioned, picking up a bigger box to wrap.

"I think most men listen with their egos and not their ears."

"Hmm. Interesting point. I guess you could say the same for the women that listen with their heart, right?"

My lips parted into a grin that he matched. "I plead the fifth."

"I bet you do." He snickered.

By the time we were finished, there was about twelve neatly wrapped gifts under the tree. I'd wrapped four of the twelve, and he did the rest. Enzo stood, marveling over his work.

"Now that's how you do it," I said from the floor with my hand up for him to slap me five.

He took my hand and pulled me up from the floor. "Thank you," he said, looking down at me.

"Mmhmm," was all I could make out. "I... I'm going to head back to sleep."

"Aight. Good night... again."

He released me, and I bid him good night before walking briskly back into the guest bedroom and closing the door behind me. The seat of my panties was moist, as I stood against the door.

"I gotta get out this man house before I end up being the gift that keeps on giving."

---

THE NEXT MORNING, I awoke to my Sunday alarm. I expected to wake up panicked, but to my surprise, I was at ease. My body felt light, thanks to the good night's rest. There was no throbbing between my legs, an indication that Enzo wasn't a creep and hadn't taken my goodies in my sleep. Although he didn't give weirdo, I slept with my legs tightly closed. Wondering what came of the snowstorm, I got out of bed and walked over to the window.

Pushing the curtain back just enough to peek out, I saw nothing but white. Everything was covered with snow. Enzo hadn't lied, and I was glad I stayed. As I stood at the window, taking everything in, he came into view. He was off to the side of the house with a big coat on, a beanie, and boots, shoveling. I watched him from the window longer than I meant to. And as if he'd felt me staring, his head lifted, and he turned to me.

Our eyes met through the glass. My stomach flipped, seeing that I was caught. Not wanting to be weird, I raised my hand and gave a small wave. He winked at me and continued working. I sucked in a breath and stepped back from the window.

"What the hell was that?" I whispered to myself, referring to the high school moment. "Girl, get it together."

Shaking my head, I grabbed my emergency kit from my purse. It was a little pouch that I traveled with in the event I found myself in a situation such as this. It consisted of a toothbrush, toothpaste, floss, a mini skin care set, and wipes. I hated being unprepared. It gave me anxiety to the highest level. Life had taught me to stay ready, so I never had to get ready.

Grabbing my phone on the way to the bathroom, I set it on the counter, while I brushed my teeth. As I went to wash my face, I could hear the door to the room open. I poked my head out of the bathroom to see EJ standing in the doorway, rubbing his eyes. On his feet was a pair of *Cars* slippers, and his durag was off.

"Good morning, sleepyhead," I said softly while wiping the facial cleanser off my face.

"Morning, Tyri. I hungry."

I laughed. "Already? You just woke up."

He just nodded.

"You eat like a grown man. I got you. Let me finish up here."

"Okay. I help you."

Smiling, I lifted him easily and set him on the sink, while I finished up. "Here, put this back in that bag please." I handed him the small toothbrush and toothpaste and pointed to the bag. I watched him squint, checking the contents of the bag, before tossing the items in. This kid was too much.

He watched as I flossed, flashing his teeth in the mirror. "Teet, Tyri."

"I see. You have nice teeth. We can brush yours once I'm done."

As I finished up, my phone rang on the counter. It was an incoming FaceTime call from KJ. Swiping the screen to answer, his face popped up on the screen. Before I could say hello, EJ leaned over into the screen like someone had called for him.

"Not you being nosey," I teased, moving him back from the screen, so I could see. **"Wassup, son?"**

**"Who kid?"** KJ asked.

**"My client's. I started that nanny position, remember?"**

**"Oh, right."** EJ looked at the screen again. **"Wassup, man?"** KJ spoke to him, and EJ gave him a head nod.

**"You alright?"** I asked KJ.

**"Yeah. I was calling to see if I can stay over Godma Nae's house for another night. Winter Break started, so I don't have school tomorrow."**

I thought for a second. **"Yeah. That's cool. Do you have practice tomorrow?"**

**"Yeah."**

**"Okay. Danae can drop you off, and I'll be there to pick you up."**

**"Ma, come on."**

**"Text me the time, KJ."**

He sucked his teeth and shook his head. **"Aight, man."**

Just then, Enzo's voice echoed outside of the bedroom, calling EJ's name.

**"I gotta go. Don't forget to text me the time,"** I said, letting EJ down off the sink. **"I love you."**

**"Uh huh. Love you too."**

I ended the call just as EJ sprinted out of the room, toward his father's voice. I stayed back, packing the rest of my toiletries away.

"Thyri, you decent?" I heard Enzo.

I walked out of the bathroom. "Yeah. Just finished brushing my teeth. How'd you make out with the snow?"

"Good. The driveway and the side are clear. Here's your car keys. I pulled it out of the garage for you." He handed me my keys and purposely brushed his hand across mine as he pulled back.

There was that feeling again, the same one from when we first met back at his office building.

"Thank you for your hospitality. The big man says he's hungry. I can make him some oatmeal before I head out."

"That'll work. Let me go get him ready for the day, and I'll set him up at the table for you."

"Okay. I'm right behind you."

Leaving the room, I passed him, making my way to the kitchen to work on breakfast. I was halfway through stirring the oatmeal when my phone rang on the counter. People usually didn't call me early on a Sunday morning. Figuring it was important, I turned the stove on low and picked it up to answer. The name Theresa, CNA came up on the screen.

Theresa was one of the CNAs at the rehab that I'd personally given my number after seeing how she tended to my father once while I was visiting. She was one of the few nursing assistants that were outsourced when Parker Jewish was short staffed. I hadn't seen her in a while, so I was curious as to why she was calling.

**"Hello?"**

**"Hey, Thyri. It's Theresa from Parker Jewish."**

**"Hey, Theresa. I know. I have your number saved. How are you?"**

**"I'm good."** She paused. **"I wanted to give you a call because I'm back at Parker for a couple days, and thankfully, I was assigned to your dad."** She cleared her throat, and then, her voice came through again quietly. **"I'm technically not supposed to be doing this, but if it were my father, I'd want someone to care enough to tell me."**

**"Wait, what's wrong with my father?"** I asked, stepping away from the stove.

**"He's regressing,"** she admitted. **"They're not gonna tell you because so long as they have an insurance to charge, they'll let the people here just waste away. Your father wants to get better; you can tell by the way he tries his best to communicate and move on his own. Unfortunately, his mobility is declining again since the last time I was here. He's also developing a bed sore. I'm not su..."**

**"A bed sore?!"** I shrieked. **"Nobody told me shit about a bed sore. How the hell did I miss that?"** I turned around with my hand on my head and found Enzo and EJ standing at the entryway of the kitchen. I muted my phone to apologize. "I'm sorry. It's my..."

"You good," Enzo assured. "EJ, go to your room real quick."

Instead of listening to his father's instruction, EJ ran over to me and hugged my leg. My vision blurred, and my hand instantly went to his back.

"Tyri, you cry."

"Come on, man." Enzo pulled him away. "She'll be aight."

**"Thyri?"** Theresa called out on the other end.

Unmuting my phone, I replied. **"Yes. I'm here."**

**"I think it would be best if you moved him and soon. I know it won't be super easy but do the best you can. I'll look out for him while I'm here. I've already started treating the sore with some cream I keep on hand, another thing I'm not supposed to do and could get fired for. But I don't give a damn. I'm gonna take care of my patients."**

**"Thank you for calling, Theresa."** My voice cracked. **"I appreciate you looking out. And this phone call will stay between you and I."**

**"Thank you. Good luck with everything. And if you ever need to hire in home care, I do that on the side. Just give me a call and we can see what works."**

**"Okay. I will."**

When the call ended, I turned back to the stove and watched the oatmeal as it bubbled. I didn't know what to do first. I felt like I was failing my father by not having an emergency plan in place for him. But plan or no plan, I had to get him out of Parker Jewish asap. I felt a presence behind me and glanced down to see Enzo's tattooed hand reach around me to turn off the eye on the stove.

"What's going on with your pops?" he asked calmly, moving on the side of me.

"That was one of the nursing assistants. She said that he's regressing and suggested that I move him asap. These mothafuckas charge his insurance all this money, and there's no adequate rehabilitation being done. I was working on a plan to set him up at home, but I need more time." I sighed and pinched the bridge of my nose. "After that call, it's clear that time is not on my side. I need to get him outta there."

The tears spilled down my cheeks before I could stop them. Crying in front of a stranger was foreign to me. I usually held my composure so well, but this was tough.

Enzo didn't hesitate to respond. "Let's go get him then. Let me make a call."

I barely had time to react before he pulled out his phone and stepped away. I could hear him talking. His voice was low, controlled, and boss like.

**"Hey, Aunty Fawn. I need a favor... I need a bed at Sullivan Manor... any openings? Yeah, I know about the wait list, but your nephew needs this."** He glanced over at me, and I attempted to wipe the tears that refused to stop. **"It's an emergency. You can bill me later... Aight, cool. I'm gonna give the phone to someone, and they're gonna give you the information."**

He walked back over with his phone held out to me. "Here, this is my Aunt Fawn. She owns a private rehab facility. Give her your dad's info, and she'll handle everything on her end."

I stared down at the phone then back at him. "It's straight. Trust me."

**"Hello?"**

**"Hi, my name is Fawn Sullivan. Who am I speaking to?"**

**"Thyri Anderson."**

**"Okay, baby. And what's the name of the patient?"**

**"My father's name is Derrick Anderson. His birthday is 11/27/19..."**

**"1964."** She finished my sentence. **"Ummm."** Her breathing sounded a little labored.

**"Hello? You okay?"** I asked, and Enzo's brow shot up.

**"Yes. Yes, I'm fine. Is your father Poppa D?"**

**"Yeah. That's his nickname,"** I said, wiping at my eyes again. **"You know him?"**

**"I could never forget my first love. Please give Enzo all**

your father's information, including the rehab he's in, so I can call over and arrange transportation. They'll need you to sign him out. It's gonna be AMA. That means against medical advice. But don't worry about that. We're gonna make sure he gets all the care he needs here at Sullivan Manor. Jesus, I can't believe this."

If she thought she was surprised, imagine mine hearing her mention my father being her first love. I had questions, but they weren't important right now.

"Okay. Thank you so much for this. I'm actually gonna head to the facility now."

"Great. And you're very welcome, love."

I handed Enzo back his phone, while I went to gather my things.

"Alright, Aunty. Good looking out."

"Thank you for calling in that favor," I said, walking back over to him. "I'm texting my father's information over to you now. I'm gonna repay you. Just let me know the cost."

"Consider it a Christmas bonus that you can't decline."

"Enzo, I can't."

"It's already done. Hit me once you get things situated, aight? If you need anything before then, hit me."

Without warning, I hugged him. He wrapped one arm around my waist, and the other rubbed my back. "Y'all in good hands. We Sullivans take good care of people."

I let him hold me for a little bit longer, appreciating the safety of his embrace. Exhaling, I pulled away. "Thank you."

"All good."

Leaving his place, I felt confident about the help I was getting. It didn't feel like it would be tied to any expectations. A part of me felt like even if it was, it wouldn't be something I'd be against.

CHAPTER 8

# A Hitta's Heart

I sat on the counter in the kitchen of my soon to be victim's home, dressed in all black, playing Solitaire like I had a right to be here. I'd played two games and had won both, so I was feeling patient, unlike the other times when I went on a hit. Time didn't move the same when you were waiting to cut someone's lifespan short. The irony of it all was the wait felt similar to the time it took for someone to be brought into the world. When I got this job, I knew I had to make a home visit.

The inside of the house told a whole different story than what I was provided on paper. Inside, there were family portraits on the walls in the hallway and above the fireplace in his great room. There were Christmas cards from his kids held up by magnets and kid's drawings that displayed their artistry.

I heard the front door open, followed by footsteps and the victim humming what sounded like a Christmas song off-key. I always found it irresponsible the way people with money didn't invest in high level security alarms to ensure their family's safety. This guy had no security in place. Good for me. A lesson he wouldn't live to learn for him. Hearing his footsteps coming my way, I tucked my phone in my hoodie and looked up in the darkness.

When the light flickered on, he froze, seeing me casually seated on his kitchen countertop.

"You know," I started to speak, "judging from the family portraits around here, one wouldn't peg you as a weirdo who took stuff that doesn't belong to them."

His mouth opened and closed in shock. I watched as his eyes darted toward the hallway, likely trying to figure out how he could escape.

"Who the fuck are you, and how'd you get in my house?!" His tone was elevated but came out bitchier than I was sure he intended it to.

I hopped down off the counter. "They call me Ezzy," I answered. "Some call me the red beam guy. Some refer to me as the one who shows up when all options have been exhausted." I took a step toward him. "That's the current case with you."

He went to take a step back, and I pulled my gun, pointing it at his head.

"You've been arrested for rape a few times," I continued in an even tone. "But somehow, the charges never stick."

His face twisted. "I don't know what the fu..."

"Luckily," I cut in, "for your last victim, these bullets will."

Lowering the gun, I hit him seven times in the chest as per the contract's orders. Each bullet landed with precision and intention.

Seven women.

Seven families lives altered.

Seven bullets were fitting.

After the deed was done, I cleaned up behind myself. I wiped down surfaces and checked corners before walking out the same way I came in – through the front door. The cool air hit me, as I stepped outside. On the way to my car, I sent the confirmation message.

Me: It's done. Push the remainder.

Getting into my car, I pulled off my hospital booties that covered my boots and tossed them into a shopping bag that sat in the passenger seat. After making my usual stop, I hopped on the highway to head home. As I drove, Thyri crossed my mind. It had been two days since she'd left the house, and EJ had been asking for her like she was a part of his daily schedule. Knowing the urgency of the situation with her father, I didn't rush her return. I knew that getting him settled was her main focus. With her fresh on my mind, I decided to give her a call.

She answered on the second ring. **"You're going to live a long time,"** she said. **"I was just thinking about calling you."**

**"Oh, word?"**

**"Yeah. I wanted to check on EJ."**

**"Crazy you say that because he's been looking for you. You made a great first impression. Now he's been waking up and checking the room you slept in like you're his human elf on the shelf."**

She laughed. **"Awww. I'ma come by and see him."**

**"How's your dad?"**

**"He's good."** She released a sigh of relief. **"He's settling in at Sullivan. I mean, they were on it as soon as transportation brought him. And guess what – your aunt and my father know each other from back in the day. Apparently, they were a thing in high school. Like a big thing. He even recognized her when he saw her. Called her Sweetie. I guess it's a nickname he had for her back then. She's been really accommodating. Even helping me put together a complaint on Parker Jewish."**

**"That's Aunty for you. She don't play about her patients. I wonder if your dad was the reason she never got married."** I thought about my aunt being with my Uncle Rodney for years before he died but never marrying him. I never asked, and on the outside looking in, they were happy with their relationship as it was. Now to hear about how she reacted to seeing Thyri's father, maybe he was the reason why.

**"I don't know. I'ma try to get the tea from Daddy, and I'll get back to you on that."** She snickered.

"**Mannn, I don't be doing that gossipin' shit. You talkin' bout 'gettin' the tea'.**" I shook my head, and she laughed.

"**Oh, please. You know you wanna know what happened. But on another note. Thank you again for making this happen though.**"

"**No thanks needed. I'm a fixer. It's what I do.**" I thought about the body that I'd just left in Queens that made my statement ring true.

"**Well, Mr. Fixer, help me with this. I'm out shopping for some last minute gifts for KJ. Any suggestions for male cologne similar to what you had on during the interview at your office?**"

"**So, you was sniffing a nigga?**"

"**Enzo, please.**" She laughed. "**I was not sniffing you, but I do have a nose.**"

"**I had on YSL Myself. The good shit.**"

"**Okay. I'll pick that up.**"

I pulled up in front of my house as the call was still going, and a text message popped up on the dashboard. It was my cousin, Kyiris, reminding me that the Christmas party was tonight, and she didn't wanna hear anything about me not coming.

"**Damn,**" I said out loud.

"**What happened?**"

"**Nothing serious. I purposely forgot about my family's annual Secret Santa Christmas party tonight and thought I'd be able to get away with it, but my cousin just reminded me about it. I pulled her name for Secret Santa, and I ain't even make it to the mall.**"

"**Oh. I can pick something up and bring it to you if you want.**"

"**Nah. You're out doing your thing. I don't wanna take you from that.**"

"**Enzo, I can do it.**" Something in the way she offered her help made me wanna do it to her. "**It's the least I can do. Tell me what she likes.**"

"Perfume for sure. That's her shit. I have her buy all my colognes."

"Okay. I got you. I'll call you when I'm on the way."

Before I could end the call, a thought popped in my head. **"Aye, Thyri, you and KJ doing anything later?"**

**"Ummm, I'll be wrapping gifts, and KJ will be avoiding me like the Black Plague. Why? Wassup? You need me for EJ?"**

I started to say, *No, I need you for me,* but it came out as an invitation instead. **"Come out to the Christmas party. I know it's late notice, but I'd like for you and KJ to join us. I got a few lil' cousins his age, so he don't have to be under you either. He can vibe out with his age group."**

**"Okay,"** she said without pause or hesitation.

**"Cool,"** I replied. **"You can dress casual."**

**"Sounds good. Talk later."**

**"Aight."**

The line went dead, but I sat in the driveway a few seconds longer.

## CHAPTER 9

# A Party With The Sullivans

By the time I left the mall, my arms were burning, and I'd decided that my last minute shopping days were over. Between the long lines and the fighting over sales, celebrating Kwanzaa didn't sound too bad. My trunk was packed with a little bit of something for everyone. I'd picked up a few body care products to send to my mother and sister, a skincare set that Danae kept hinting at, a robe, slippers, and shaving kit for my dad, and a car set for EJ that I couldn't pass up. I even walked out with something for Enzo because it just felt like the right thing to do.

Time had gotten the best of me, so I had to change courses at the last minute. I texted Enzo that I wouldn't be able to make it to see EJ and asked if it would be okay if I brought the gift I'd picked up for his cousin to the party. He agreed, letting me know that there was no rush for me to get there and to drive safe.

I thought that was cute. Him inviting me and KJ to his family gathering was cute too, considering that he'd been heavy on my mind the past two days. His generosity spoke volumes, and I wanted to thank him ten times over for aiding in the transfer of my father. Watching a man spring into action while you were in distress and actually get shit done meant a lot.

Sullivan Manor was beautiful. I could tell that his aunt had put a lot of thought into the place, from the decor and cleanliness, down to the way you were greeted on arrival. Parker Jewish didn't hold a candle to all Ms. Fawn had going on at Sullivan Manor. It was clear that my father had gone from the projects to the penthouse of rehab centers.

Ms. Fawn gave me the full layout and had a treatment plan in place for my dad that I was fully on board with. She even let me know that she would personally see to it that my father was doing his PT three times a week and walking daily. I caught the twinkle in her eye when she spoke to my father and the way she rubbed his hand lovingly. She still had a thing for her high school sweetheart, and I was sure that once my daddy was back at one hundred percent, he'd be back to his same charming self.

Finally making it home, I balanced the bags on both of my arms and shouldered the door open. When I walked in, I could see KJ pacing the living room floor with his head down. His phone was in his hand on speaker, and by the way he was burning a hole in my floor, I could tell the conversation wasn't pleasant. I already knew who was on the other end before I heard his voice.

**"Dad, what I..."**

**"No,"** Kaleb interjected, **"this is the part where you shut the fuck up."** His voice was sharp and tight. Whatever KJ had done really had him pissed off. **"Just the other day, I'm tellin' ya moms that she need to give you some room to bump your head as young men do when growing up, then you go and do some dumb shit, and for what. KJ?"**

**"I didn't even do it."**

**"But you were going to, right?"**

Silence.

**"Exactly. Don't play me, KJ. You can't play a nigga that already been in the game. I've been your age. You ain't been mine."**

I closed the door behind me, and KJ's head shot up, freezing mid-step.

**"Is your mother there?"**

KJ hesitated before letting him know that I was and walked

over to hand the phone to me. Setting the bags down at my feet, I took it.

"What happened?" I asked him, and he just walked away.

**"Oohhhkay. So, I'm assuming you're gonna tell me what happened,"** I said with the phone attached to my ear and my body heating up from nervousness.

**"I'm not gonna go into detail because I handled it."** Kaleb's tone had shifted. It was still heated but more controlled now that I was on the line.

**"Really, Kaleb? KJ has two parents."**

**"Yeah, well, just like you didn't feel the need to tell me you went to The Bronx late as hell to get him, I don't feel the need to divulge this. What I will say is if he's not at school, practice, or Danae crib, that lil' nigga is to be home until I say otherwise."**

**"That don't tell me nothin', Kaleb."**

**"Ain't shit to tell other than what I said. I handled it. All I need you to do is be on board with what I just told you. Tell him I'm gonna call him tomorrow."**

The line went dead before I could say anything else.

"Rude ass," I griped. I hated not being able to have the last word.

I sat EJ's, Enzo's, and his cousin's gifts in the living room and headed to my bedroom to put the others away for wrapping later. Taking my coat off, I walked down the hall to KJ's room. It was cracked, like he knew I was on my way, but I still knocked.

"Come in, Ma."

I pushed the door open, and he was laid out on his bed, tossing his basketball up in the air.

"So, I'm not gonna ask what happened because your father made it very clear that it's between you and him."

He sat up and looked at me with a raised brow.

"Hey," I threw my hands up, "sometimes I know when to back down. He said he handled it, so that's what it is. But he also was very clear that if you're not at school, Danae's, or practice, you're home. Pretty much what's already in place."

He huffed. "I guess I can tell my friend it's a dub for the party he invited me to."

"You guessed rightttt!" I yelled out like a game show host, only he didn't find shit funny. "But I'm glad you brought up party."

He frowned. "Why?"

"Cause we were invited to one. And you're going. And we're gonna match."

"Oh, nahhhhh." He waved his hands dramatically.

"Okay, I dragged that last part," I said, laughing. "But the part about you coming, I meant that. So, go head and throw something on so you can step witcha mom."

"Wait. Can I at least know whose party it is since you forcing me to go?"

I smiled. "Shower and change. We're leaving soon."

He stared at me, as I two stepped at his door, and shook his head. I saw a piece of a smile breaking through before he got up and headed for his bathroom.

And just like that, whatever tension there was in the air from his phone call with his father had loosened enough to get him moving. I had high hopes for tonight. He'd thank me later.

<hr>

As I TURNED onto the block that Enzo had given me the address to, things started to look familiar. I thought nothing of the address until this very moment. We got closer, and the parking lot was packed with all kinds of luxury cars. Some cars were double parked, while others were in designated spots, separated by valet cones. As we drove farther in, a guy, who I assumed was security, directed us to a spot in the second row of the lot. This shit was a whole production.

KJ leaned forward in his seat. "Nahhh. This where the party at?" He pointed out, amused. "The diner?"

"Yes. The one Danae works at. This is so wild to me." I

glanced up, and the words SULLIVAN DINER lit up in big, red letters.

We'd visited the diner a few times to eat but not since Danae got her promotion. I would've never thought to put two and two together.

"Lemme call her." I dialed Danae's number, and she answered on the first ring.

**"What you doing at my job, heffa? I told you I don't work tonight."**

We all shared locations, so she knew exactly where we were.

**"I'm here for a holiday party that Enzo invited me to... with his family!"**

**"Wait, Enzo is a Sullivan? Girl, the world ain't never been that small. And wait, now I'm offended because I was banned from coming to the party and the family love me."**

**"Who banned you?"**

**"Girl, Aura crazy ass. Talkin' bout if I come to the party and I'm not his date, it's gon' be a problem. He don't want nobody thinkin' his woman single. Losin' me so bad."**

**"Oh, he's a looney toon."** I cackled.

**"No. He's delusional and calculating as fuck. Then, he got the nerve to be the boss and finer than a mothafucka. It's a deadly combination. That's why I'm not giving in to his persistence. He's an arrest warrant waiting to happen. You know I'm certified."**

**"I thought you said his sister owns the diner?"** I asked, puzzled.

**"She does. They own a whole bunch of shit. When I say he's the boss, I mean the boss of all bosses."**

**"Ohhhh,"** I dragged out, picking up what she was putting down. **"Got it. Well, you need to come out anyway in case me and KJ get outnumbered."**

KJ snickered in the passenger seat.

"Why you laughin'?"

"Cause this the same party Cortez invited me to. And he's a Sullivan."

I blinked. "You lyin'."

"Nah. Forreal. Look."

He held up his phone where he had a text thread going with his friend, Cortez. KJ had let him know that he couldn't make it and said something slick about me that made me side eye him quickly. Of course, like any teenager trying to get over, Cortez suggested letting me know that it was a family gathering at his aunt's diner.

**"This is insane,"** I said, sitting back in disbelief.

**"See,"** Danae said, **"everybody know everybody. Lemme get dressed. I'ma bout to come up there. Fuck what Aura talkin' bout. What color y'all got on, so we can match?"**

"Ahhh, hell na," KJ groaned, and we both cracked up laughing.

"Watch your mouth." I playfully mushed him. **"We'll see you in a minute, D."**

**"Okay."**

I hung up, still laughing. Texting Enzo that we had arrived, I grabbed my purse and stepped out of the car to put my fur on. I guess I was looking too good in my jumpsuit because instead of walking ahead of me like he normally did, KJ walked on the side of me, close like we were Siamese twins. He didn't know it, but I loved it.

From the outside, I could see that the diner had been completely transformed. The place was lit up, and I could see a big tree that I could bet was real, standing in front of the window. As we made it up the steps, the door opened, and a heavyset man dressed in all black held his hand out to stop us. The bass from the music let me know they were inside having a ball.

KJ leaned over and whispered in my ear. "They take they Christmas parties seriously."

Before I could nod, the security spoke. "You have an in..."

"They good, Mack." Although I couldn't see him behind the overgrown security, I knew Enzo's voice. "They with me," he added calmly.

Big guy stepped aside immediately.

"Come on in," Enzo instructed. Holding the door open for us, he gave me a light peck on the cheek and held his hand out to KJ. "KJ, right?"

"The one and only," KJ confirmed smoothly. They shook hands firmly, showing mutual respect.

I had half expected him to be standoffish, so I was pleasantly surprised by his greeting.

The place was packed with people but not too bad to where the air felt thick and people were rubbing elbows. Enzo offered to take our coats, and before we could hand them over, a voice shouted through the crowd.

"Nigga! I thought you said ya moms said you couldn't come. Yo' lyin' ass." A tall boy who I recognized as Cortez made his way through the crowd. "Oh – my bad, Ms. Anderson," he said once he realized KJ wasn't alone. "How you doin'? You look nice. I like that red."

"Aye, nigga." KJ pushed him back.

I smiled. "Hey, Cortez. I'm good and thank you."

Enzo reached out and mushed his head. "Watch how you approach adults, lil' nigga."

Cortez laughed. "Aight, cuzzo. C'mon, bro." He slung his arm around KJ's neck, and they disappeared into the crowd.

I handed Enzo my coat, and he grabbed my hand to guide me through the crowd. We went through a bunch of friendly smiles. His family, both old and young, were dancing, laughing, drinking, and eating. It was a vibe for sure. I took it all in, loving the feeling of being amongst family. Pulling the chain to my purse out of my bag to wear it crossbody, I went to put it over my head when I felt a small body crash into my leg.

"Tyriiii!"

I looked down to find EJ wrapped around my leg.

"Ahhh, look at my boy!" I laughed, bending down to pick him up. "Wassup, dude?"

He laughed as I tickled him. I completely tuned Enzo out, as EJ started to give me the rundown of what he'd been doing in two-year-old English. Enzo laughed, asking EJ if it was okay if he let me meet everybody. He nodded and went back to talking like Enzo had interrupted his flow.

Not only was I introduced to everyone, but Enzo also moved me through the room like I belonged there. Me, his nanny. I met his cousins, aunts, uncles, distant family members, and even his mom. She'd picked up on the way EJ clung to me throughout the party, refusing to leave my side.

"Look at him." His mother pointed out. "You got your own personal bodyguard."

"No, forreal," one of his cousins added. "We ain't had to stop the party to look for him or nothin'," he joked. "You just might be the one, Thyri."

I smiled, glancing down at EJ, who held onto my leg with one hand and busied himself with Enzo's phone in the other.

"This my guy," I said.

"Alright, alright," someone spoke from a microphone. "It's time for The Sullivan Family Holiday Games. Y'all got five minutes to get y'all teams together. And I'm setting a timer. Go!"

People rushed to tables, putting their teams together. And they didn't discriminate. I saw the seniors grabbing a few teenagers and the little kids to their team. Just watching them told me everything I needed to know – this family was competitive as hell.

"Ma, Aura, Shawna, KJ, Brandi, and Cortez, y'all on my team," Enzo announced.

KJ and Cortez ran over to us and sat at our table along with the rest of our teammates. We played a few trivia games that included Charades, Heads Up, and Lyrically Correct. I got us a win in Lyrically Correct. Beat the people so bad, they thought I was cheating. And then it got serious with games that involved movement and speed, which I shamelessly lost.

I was having so much fun, a couple hours had slipped by before I even noticed. As the games came to an end, I got a text from Danae, letting me know that she was walking inside. I got excited like I hadn't seen my cousin in years. I spotted her, as she entered the diner in a two- piece, leather set and a cropped fur coat. Before I could wave her over, Aura called out her name. She went to duck, but he was on her like a bee to honey.

"You know ya cousin be harassing my cousin, right?" I said to Enzo, who was watching the party from his seat.

"Danae yo' people?"

I nodded.

"Oh, he in love with that girl," he said like it was a known thing.

"So, y'all get crazy when y'all in love, huh?"

He nodded slowly. "And very territorial. But we loyal as fuck and protect with our lives."

Turning away from him, I made a mental note of that. The night continued on with Aura finally freeing my cousin and allowing her to mingle. We turned the dance floor up with the other women in the family. From the old school classics to the new Tik Tok trends, me and Danae were on it. I just knew KJ was somewhere fighting the air. Not only was his mother fine, but I kept in touch with what was in.

There was another announcement, this time for the gift exchange. Remembering that I'd left Enzo's gift that he was supposed to give his cousin in the car, I let him know that I was going to get it.

"Hold on, I'm coming witchu."

EJ looked up at me and grabbed my hand.

"I guess he is too." I giggled.

Enzo went to grab our coats, and we walked outside with EJ in the middle of us. I unlocked the door as we got close and directed Enzo to the backseat to grab the gift.

"All three or just this one?" he questioned before closing the door and holding up the small gift bag for him while clutching EJ's gift under his arm. "What's this?"

I smiled and shrugged lightly. "Consider it a gift you can't decline."

For a second, he didn't say anything. Then, he closed what little distance there was between us and spoke. "Thank you. You didn't have to."

"I wanted to," I replied confidently.

The moment settled between us before he leaned in and kissed my lips. It was gentle with a little hunger in it. Before either of us could take the kiss up a notch, EJ hit both our legs. I laughed at us almost forgetting the little person we had with us.

"Tyri," he called out to me with his lips poked out.

"Awwww," I cooed and bent down, so he could kiss my cheek. "Thank you so much."

Enzo chuckled. "That's wild, EJ. You don't share women with Daddy."

EJ nodded, making us both laugh, as we headed back inside.

I didn't know what the kiss meant. What I did know was that anything felt possible in the moment, and the Sullivans knew how to throw a party.

## CHAPTER 10

# The Kid Knows

A week had passed since the Christmas party, and Thyri had become the subject of the family group chat. It seemed that everyone had picked up on her vibe and was drawn to her. Even my aunts talked about KJ and how he blended in with the other teenagers in my family. Everything was cool up until they started taking polls on how long it would take before I was locked down. I couldn't have exited the chat any faster.

I'd thought about that night a few times. The way EJ wouldn't leave her side. The cologne she'd gifted me. And the kiss outside her car that would've had her fucked had EJ not been around. She'd watched EJ three times since then, and when she wasn't at the house, we were on the phone. Whether text or Face-Time, we spoke at least twice a day. The conversations had begun to carry a little weight with me too. It was to the point where if I didn't hear from her, I wanted to know what she was doing.

Let Aura tell it, it wouldn't be too long before I was on her like he was on her cousin. I had to remind him that there were no words for his method of courting. That nigga could go from cool to bat shit crazy if he didn't get his way. I didn't know how Danae dealt with it in the capacity that she did.

Christmas was a day away, and Sullivan & Co. had been on a holiday run. Orders were coming in back-to-back, especially from venues that were hosting holiday parties. The ladies had worked twice over to reach our goal of doubling our sales from last year, and we'd done that and some. I sat in my office, going over the books and signing off on bonus checks, while Thyri and EJ kept me company on FaceTime.

**"Tell me why me and your son got into it today."**

**"Over what?"** I laughed.

**"Him getting mad because I whooped him in Connect Four twice."**

**"He probably got mad because he can't play. You probably cheated my boy like KJ did me on that 2K. He still gotta run that back."**

**"Oh, so you and yo' son some sore losers? Cause me and my boy won those games fair and square."**

After seeing how well KJ got along with my little cousins at the party, I'd convinced Thyri to ease up a little on the punishment he was on, granting him a few hours of leisure when she was at my house watching EJ. She agreed, so long as the leisure was in the house. So far, he'd been cool, hanging out with my cousins at Kyiris' crib, which was only ten minutes down the road from me. She'd taken a liking to Thyri and assured her that KJ was safe with her and had given Thyri the okay to come by at any time to check in. Her place was where all the kids convened because she didn't have kids of her own. Everyone was always safe and welcomed.

**"Man, whatever."** I waved her off. **"Let me finish up here, and I'll be headed in to relieve you of your duties."**

**"Okay. Hurry up. You told EJ we would bake these cookies before I go, and you know he's waiting up to see to it that it's done."**

**"Aight, boss."**

Ending the call, I finished going over the books and signing off on the last bonus check. I called the ladies into the conference room through the AP system I had installed, and they all came to the door, all knocking at once.

"Damn, y'all must know I got some money in here." I

laughed, walking over to open the door to ten smiles. "Y'all look goofy as hell."

They all giggled, filing in.

"Where da bag at, nigga, where da bag at?" Chatoria, one of my best cleaners, sang with her hand out.

"You a lil' thirsty for two hundred extra dollars." The smiles on their faces dropped, and everyone instantly got serious before I burst out laughing.

"That's not even funny, Enzo." Kalia swatted at me.

"Yoooo, I was about to say. Ever since he done got his lil' girl-friend/nanny, he been actin' unusual," Chatoria let out with a smirk.

"Stay out my business, woman." I handed her her envelope first and went down the line with the others. Leaning back on my desk, I watched them each open their envelopes. "I want y'all to know Sullivan & Co. don't run without y'all. This is just a small token of my appreciation."

Inside the envelopes were $5,000 checks. By the look on their faces, I could tell they didn't expect that level of generosity. But I fucked with my staff more than they knew.

Chatoria teared up, walking over to me with her arms outstretched. "Hug me, nigga."

"Yo ass is crazy." I chuckled, standing up to hug her. And of course, everyone took it as an open invitation. A slew of thank you's and I love you's came with it. "Yeah, yeah, love y'all too. I love y'all enough to let y'all shut the building down too. I gotta get home and relieve my nanny."

"I'm talkin' bout innatttttt," Chatoria chanted.

Shutting down my computer, I grabbed my phone. "Good night, y'all. Text the group chat once y'all make it home. Whoever don't text, that's y'all ass."

WHEN I GOT HOME, I could smell the double chocolate chip

cookies from the door. Thryi and EJ had started baking without me.

"Ahhh, y'all bogus as hell," I said, walking in the kitchen and finding them at the island eating the leftover cookie dough out the bowl.

Thyri giggled. "I tried to wait for you, but he wore me down. We sorry. Look, EJ, do this." She coached EJ into a sad face to which he'd mastered long ago.

"Sowwy, Daddy."

"Ion even wanna hear it."

"Awww, he mad. Let's give him a hug, EJ."

EJ stood up on the counter with his bare feet and walked over to me, while she hugged me from the side.

"Y'all still bogus," I said to the both of them.

"Daddy, kiss," he encouraged, pushing mine and Thyri's heads together.

"Gentle, EJ," she spoke softly.

He listened, slowly pushing our heads together. Thyri smiled and let me kiss her twice.

"Oh, it's cool when you initiate it, huh?"

EJ grinned and went back to work on the cookie dough.

"I think he fuckin' wit' our drip. What you think?"

"I think kids can feel when things are right. So, I'ma go with that." She kissed the side of my mouth then turned to the stove.

Once the cookies were done, we ate a few of them and watched *Cars* with EJ until he fell asleep at eleven.

"Okay. I gotta get outta here and get home before twelve. Me and KJ have this thing where we open a gift at midnight. We've been doing it since he was five, and I can't mess up the tradition."

I helped her up from the floor and pulled her into a hug before walking her out to her car.

"This job turned out to be more than I expected," she said. "I'm looking forward to seeing how this plays out both professionally and personally."

"Fasho. There's always another page to every story. Merry Christmas Eve, shorty."

"Merry Christmas Eve, Enzo."


THE END... FOR NOW
TURN TO THE NEXT PAGE FOR A COVER REVEAL TO
THE STORY THAT WILL GIVE YOU MORE FROM
THESE CHARACTERS. AND I'M NOT JUST TALKING
ABOUT THYRI & ENZO.


HAPPY HOLIDAYS, FINE SHII, AND LET US NOT
FORGET... I DON'T WANNA ARGUE!

WHEN LOVE CLAIMS
A DEADLY SOUL.

KEEP ME IN

MIND

a black mafia romance

NAI

# Did You Enjoy?

Did you enjoy the read?
Let us know how much by leaving us a
review on Amazon and Goodreads.

# Other Books By
## URBAN AINT DEAD

Tales 4rm Da Dale

The Hottest Summer Ever

Hittin' Licks For The Holidays: Atlanta

Wet Dreams On Lockdown: The Nurse

How To Publish A Book From Prison

How To Invest In The Stock Market From Prison

First Summer Out With My Prison Bae

By **Elijah R. Freeman**

Despite The Odds

Despite The Odds 2

By **Juhnell Morgan**

Hittaz

Hittaz 2

Hittaz 3

Hittaz 4

Hittaz 5

Hittaz 6

Coldhearted

Coldhearted 2

Coldhearted 3

By **Lou Garden Price, Sr.**

A YN'S Muse For The Summer

Wizdom: Forever Your Gangsta

Charge It To The Game

Charge It To The Game 2

Charge It To The Game 3

A Summer To Remember With My Hitta

Snatched Up By A Hitta

Santa Sent Me A Real One For Christmas

Wet Dreams On Lockdown: The Unit Manager

Thug Me The Right Way 2

Thug Me The Right Way 3

Seizing A Gangsta's Heart For The Summer

Yours For The Taking

Wrapped Up In A Hitta's Love For Christmas

By **Nai**

A Set Up For Revenge

A Set Up For Revenge 2

Wet Dreams On Lockdown: The Librarian

By **Ashley Williams**

Trickin' On A Heaux For Christmas

Homie Hoppin' For The Holidays

Wet Dreams On Lockdown: The Female C.O

Letters Of His Love

By **Telia Teanna**

The State's Witness

The State's Witness 2

The State's Witness 3

This Time Won't You Save Me

This Time Won't You Save Me 2

His Summer Side Piece

A Holiday Heist

Healing The Heart Of A Detroit Gangsta

Summer Vows With A Detroit Gangsta

The Promissory

The Promissory 2

A Gangsta's Last Kiss

What Do The Lonely Do At Christmas

By **Kyiris Ashley**

Stuck In The Trenches

Stuck In The Trenches 2

By **Huff Tha Great**

Melted The Heart Of A Menace

Wet Dreams On Lockdown: Lieutenant Grace

By **P. Wise**

Merry Trapmas

By **Mia Sky**

Thug Me The Right Way

By **DiamondATL & Nai**

Wet Dreams On Lockdown: The Counselor

By **Paris Iman**

Wet Dreams On Lockdown: The Male C.O

By **Tamyra Griffin**

Wet Dreams On Lockdown: The Captain

By **TN Jones**

Wet Dreams On Lockdown: The Warden

By **Shawnice**

Atlantastan

Atlantastan 2

Atlantastan 3

By **Chris Green**

IN The Streetz

IN The Streetz 2

IN The Streetz 3

IN The Streetz 4

IN The Streetz 5

IN The Streetz 6

Hittin' Licks For The Holidays: Charleston

By **Tron Hill**

Hittin' Licks For The Holidays: New York

Bandemic

Bandemic 2

By **Freshh Moneyy**

Coming Soon From
URBAN AINT DEAD

Drill
The Hottest Summer Ever 2
THE G-CODE
Tales 4rm Da Dale 2
How To Build Your Credit From Prison
By **Elijah R. Freeman**

Despite The Odds 3
By **Juhnell Morgan**

A Felon's Promise
By **Nai**

Colliding Into Your Love
**By Kyiris Ashley**

To Die For
By **Tron Hill**

Bandemic 3
**By Freshh Moneyy**